Into the
River Lands

ALSO BY SCOTT B. WILLIAMS

Fiction
The Pulse
Refuge
The Darkness After
Sailing the Apocalypse

Nonfiction
On Island Time
Paddling the Pascagoula
Exploring Coastal Mississippi
Bug Out
Bug Out Vehicles and Shelters
Getting Out Alive:
The Prepper's Workbook

ISBN-13: 978-1514740552
Cover photograph: Mississippi Woodlands © Scott B. Williams
Cover photograph: © banglds, file #28021993, fotolia
Cover and interior design: Scott B. Williams
Editor: Michelle Cleveland

Into the River Lands

Darkness After Series

Scott B. Williams

This one is for Houston,

One

APRIL GIBBS LIFTED HER paddle out of the water at the end of her stroke and let the canoe drift midstream while she tried to think. Her ex-boyfriend, David Green was in front of her in the bow seat, and it was all she could do to refrain from using the paddle to smack him so he would shut up. He wasn't helping her paddle, and he sure wasn't helping her find what she was looking for.

"I think we made a terrible mistake, April. We're never going to find that farm and now we're lost out here in the middle of the woods with nothing and no way to get back."

"We're not *lost*, David! I told you, I'm just not sure exactly which bend in the creek it is. I'll know it when I see it. That's a lot different than being lost!"

"Not if we don't find it, it isn't. What if we've already passed it and you just didn't know it? We'd never be able to paddle back upstream against this current. We'll end up who knows where if we just keep going."

"We *haven't* passed it, David. I'm certain of that. The path isn't obvious and it isn't visible from the creek. Mitch said that was deliberate. His dad didn't want just anyone floating down the creek to find the way to his land. He said they always had to keep an eye out for poachers and other trespassers. But the trail *is* there. We have to just keep stopping at every bend that looks like the one I remember, and by looking in the woods just beyond the creek we'll find the path when we're at the right one. I'm certain that it's close. I told you that I remember it being just a few miles past that last bridge we went under."

"I hope you're right, because if you're wrong, we're all going to die out here."

"We're not as likely to die out here as we were back in Hattiesburg. You know that. You saw what was happening. There's no way they can defend that building indefinitely. The whole city is a death zone. Besides, we're here now and there's no going back!"

"Maybe, but I'm still not convinced we're any better off. You don't even know if that redneck kid is even going to be there if we find his place. He may be dead by now for all we know."

"I told you not to call him that again! He may live in the woods, but he's *not* ignorant or stupid, and he's definitely not a *kid*. He's more mature than most adults of any age that I've met. And yeah, something could have happened to him, but I doubt it. You just have no idea what's he's capable of. He wouldn't do anything foolish because he's got his little sister and her friends to take care of. He'll be there, I'm sure of it."

"And I'm sure you can't wait to see him. He's still under

age and he's still too young for you, even if he does act mature!"

"Just shut up and paddle, David. All you're doing is pissing me off with your dumb comments. What I do, I do for Kimberly. She's all that matters to me anymore, but she needs us both right now, so let's just focus on that, okay?"

April was frustrated and angry, mostly with herself, but listening to David's "I told you so" smart aleck remarks most of the evening and the day before had really pushed her over the edge. She was sick of looking at him and sick of hearing him talk, but that was really nothing new. What was more infuriating was that after coming this far, and getting this close, she still hadn't found the place she was looking for. April couldn't believe how much everything out here looked the same, and nothing in particular stood out despite her having traveled this exact route just seven months before. Of course, she remembered there was pretty much nothing but trackless forest on both sides of Black Creek for mile after mile. She remembered that landmarks such as bridge overpasses were few and far between along its course, but she had not imagined it would be so hard to locate the one specific bend in the waterway she was searching for. It stood out in her memory as a bend with a low, shaded sandbar on its inside radius and a dense thicket of bay trees in the understory of the forest beyond. The problem was that they had already stopped and investigated at least nine or ten such bends that looked just like the one she remembered, and all led to nothing. There was no hidden path leading through the bay thicket away from the creek bottom, no rusty barbed-wire fence beyond, where the hardwoods transitioned to pines, and no Henley pasturelands past that. All she and David found were trees and more trees in a silent forest devoid of all sounds of human life.

Though she wanted to beat herself up for not remembering, April kept reminding herself that not only had it been seven months since she'd been here, but that it had been her one and only time to canoe *any* river. Before the events that led her here that first time with Mitch Henley, the woods to April were just a blur of greenery seen from the car window while driving down the highway. She was a city girl in her previous life, all of her nearly nineteen years of it before the world changed completely. Now, life in any city was too dangerous to consider, and living in an artificial environment in such isolation from nature was virtually impossible anyway without the endless supply chain feeding the incessant demands of the population. Reality had changed in the course of just one night when a bombardment of electromagnetic pulses from the sun shut down the power grid, along with most every modern technology from transportation to communication. Now, like everyone else lucky or resourceful enough to still be alive in the nightmare of the aftermath, April was doing what she had to do in order to survive. But above all, she was doing it for Kimberly, the eighteen-month-old daughter who was the light and the purpose of her life.

David Greene had fathered their little girl, but whatever she'd felt for him at the time that led to that event was long forgotten. He was here only because she felt that two parents were better than one, especially during such a perilous journey. She knew full well it was dangerous to travel anywhere, alone or not, but this was a journey she deemed necessary. When she'd passed this way all those months before, all that had mattered was getting *to* Kimberly. Now, with her baby sleeping quietly in a blanket between her feet in the bottom of the canoe, getting back to the Henley farmhouse was a matter of life or death. She was certain that Mitch Henley would be there, and that if anyone could keep her and Kimberly safe long enough to find out if they had a future, it was Mitch. All she had to do was find him—a task so simple and yet so hard out here in this vast river land forest he called home.

Two

MITCH HENLEY FOUND THE wounded doe collapsed in a pile of bloody leaves at the bottom of a deep ravine. Another half hour and he would have lost hope of finding the animal at all. Dusk was fading rapidly to the darker shadows of night and the sporadic blood trail was hard to follow, even for a tracker with his skills. Without hesitation, he drew his longbow and unleashed the hunting arrow that was already nocked and ready on the string, finishing a job someone else had so badly botched.

Mitch had been scouting rather than hunting that late fall afternoon, though he never left the house anymore without a weapon at the ready for just such chance opportunities as this one. He first jumped the doe while threading his way through a thicket along the creek bank on his way back home to his family land. It had been a long day of exploring and marking trails, and he was anxious to get back to the farmhouse to tell the others about an impressive stand of old-growth cypress he'd found along a hidden slough far from his normal hunting grounds.

The chill in the air had him moving faster than usual that

day, and with a little less caution than if he were seriously hunting for food. It was the first real cold of the season; a blustery north wind stirring the treetops above him, rattling branches and sending leaves and pine needles spiraling softly to the forest floor. He was ready to call it a day and get back to the warmth of the fire, and so he was momentarily startled when the small deer burst out of hiding without warning just a few yards in front of him.

Mitch knew immediately from its erratic gate and stiff hind leg that it was hurt, but there was no time for a shot before it disappeared in the undergrowth. The leaf litter where it had been resting was soaked in blood, and scattered drops left as it fled provided just enough sign for an experienced hunter to follow. But Mitch slowed down and took his time doing so, knowing if he pressed it too close the deer might still run for miles. He figured the animal had been hit in the leg or some other non-vital area, and though it would eventually bleed out and die, it might take hours. Mitch hated the thought of wounded game going to waste, and that's exactly what would happen to this deer if he didn't track it down before dark. But more than he and the others needed the meat, he needed to know who the sloppy hunter was who'd wounded it and with what kind of weapon. He hadn't heard a gunshot all day, but from the speed the deer was still able to run when he'd startled it, he doubted it had been very long since it was hit by whatever caused the bleeding.

Now that the doe's final run was over and he had caught up, he lost no time in ending the animal's suffering. When his arrow struck home, the shaft buried itself almost to the fletching in the soft neck, and no doubt would have passed all the way through if not stopped by the ground behind it. The deer would be dead or nearly dead by the time he climbed down to reach it, but out of habit, Mitch nocked another arrow, just in case. He'd been careful the whole time he was following the blood trail, stopping often to look and listen for minutes at a time—not only to avoid spooking the terrified animal into running farther—but also to stay alert for any signs of the hunter who'd started this. He hadn't heard or seen a thing, including any evidence that anyone else had attempted to find the deer, but he was much too cautious to let his guard down now. Mitch did not at all like the idea of a stranger in these woods so close to home.

He carefully made his way down the steep bank of slick red clay, using exposed roots as hand and footholds. When he reached the fallen deer it was still, but just to make sure its suffering was over, he drew his hunting knife and opened the jugular to bleed it out. Then he rolled the carcass over, searching for the source of the blood that led him here. What he found explained why he had heard no report of a rifle or shotgun. Protruding from the animal's hind quarter was some six inches of broken carbon fiber arrow shaft, the broad head tip no doubt lodged in the pelvic bone. Someone had made a lousy shot or else the deer jumped the string at the last second, not quite fast enough to avoid being hit entirely.

The lightweight composite arrow was typical of the projectiles modern sport bowhunters used with compound bows, if such high-tech machines could even be called bows. Mitch didn't like them, preferring instead his traditional longbow with its heavy, sixty-pound draw weight and no mechanical advantage to make it easier to pull, hold and aim. The simplicity of a simple stick bow, one of mankind's oldest and most effective weapons, also meant there was nothing to break but the string or the bow itself, both easy to replace from available materials. High-tech compound bows were far too dependent on complex materials and manufacturing to be viable in this new reality.

Besides, even if the bow itself held up, anyone using such a weapon now would not be doing so indefinitely. With no easy way to procure or make more arrows capable of handling the tremendous asymmetric forces generated, such technology would soon be useless. At least with his simple weapon Mitch could use primitive arrows fabricated from river cane, and there was an endless supply of that growing for the taking along the banks of Black Creek.

Satisfied with his examination as to the cause of the doe's wound, Mitch set to work with his knife to carefully open the abdominal cavity and remove the entrails, separating the heart, liver and kidneys and wrapping them in some big magnolia leaves before stashing them in his small daypack. The hunting was good in the vicinity of the Henley property and Mitch's prowess with the bow assured a steady supply of meat. But living on a largely carnivorous diet, he and the others craved the fatty and nutrient-rich organ meats that were far too precious to discard as many did in the days before the collapse. Tonight, they would eat well and he would come back for the rest of the venison tomorrow. With the cold front moving through the area, the lows would be at or near freezing before dawn, and the meat would be fine until he could pack it home.

Using a length of rope he kept in his pack, he tossed one end over a high branch and hoisted the carcass out of the reach of scavengers. He would be back for it early, but at first light in the morning, he would backtrack the blood trail from where he'd jumped the deer. Mitch intended to find out who shot that arrow and where he or she had gone afterwards. The security of everyone who depended on him to look out for them required nothing less.

Three

DAVID HAD BEEN QUIET for a good hour since their last argument, but April knew it wouldn't last long so she wasn't surprised when he started complaining again as the afternoon light faded.

"We'll never find anything in the dark, that's for sure. So what are we gonna do now?"

"Find a place to camp, that's what? What do you think we're gonna do? Kimberly is hungry and you're right, we can't keep looking in the dark. We can't take a chance of passing that trail. We'll stop at the next sandbar and start looking again in the morning."

April had quickly learned to make herself comfortable sleeping in the woods during her brief, but intense journey with Mitch Henley. Though it was only a few days they spent together, there was so much excitement, adventure and danger packed into those days it had seemed much longer. But despite the risks and the overwhelming odds they encountered, Mitch always seemed to know just what to do and he never hesitated to follow through with doing it.

April doubted she would be alive now if not for Mitch

Henley. The day he came into her life was the day that she left the blacked-out city of New Orleans in an attempt to drive north to Hattiesburg—a trip of less than two hours on a normal day. But by then, just four days after the pulse event, there *were* no normal days. Even attempting the one-hundred mile trip through the mostly rural and wooded countryside of Mississippi would have been out of the question for a city girl like her if she had no working car, like the vast majority of the stranded population. The damage caused by the pulse did not spare the electronic components that control modern engines, and most vehicles new enough to be in everyday use had rolled to a stop within seconds, coming to rest where they ran out of momentum; abandoned by their occupants soon after.

April was among the lucky few who had access to a still-running antique; David's classic 1969 Mustang that had no complex electrics and therefore was unaffected by the surge. The carburetor had been in pieces where he had been rebuilding it, but the new parts and instructions were all there. Working with determination born of desperation, April put it all back together and got the car running all by herself. She had no choice. David was not there to do it, and with him was the one thing in her life that mattered more than anything—her precious daughter, Kimberly. How could she have known when he left with her to visit his parents in Hattiesburg that the world would change forever in a matter of hours? That she would wake in the morning to no working phones, lights, computers, television or radio? That she would have no way of knowing what happened or when it was all going to be fixed, assuming like everyone else that it was simply a temporary power outage?

It took a full day for the reality to sink in and then a couple more for her to get the old Mustang running, but when she did, she got out while she could without telling a soul of her plans. Starting the car before dawn the forth day after the grid went down, she made her way through the obstacle course of stalled vehicles that clogged every route out of the city. Dodging throngs of pedestrians and nearly hitting several who stepped into her path trying to force her to stop. April gunned the hot rod V-8 and peeled rubber as she shifted gears. She was not shy about letting anyone who dared get in her way know that she would run over them before giving up the car.

Somehow, she made it out of the city and across the interstate bridge leading to Slidell without getting carjacked. The number of stalled cars and people walking the roads prompted her to leave Interstate 59 at the first opportunity however, and once across Lake Pontchartrain, she turned off to take the older route north, a two-lane highway David had shown her on one of their leisurely Sunday trips to visit his parents.

April felt a lot better about traveling Highway 11. It was much less congested even though it was smaller and only a two lane. Soon she was out of the cities and suburbs, rolling along past mixed forests and farm fields. All was well until the Mustang sputtered and then died, rolling to a stop within sight of a single, isolated farmhouse. April knew the fuel gauge didn't work, and David had run out of gas once before because of it. She had no way of knowing how much was in the tank when she left, so she was hardly surprised that it was empty now. People had said you couldn't get gas from any of the gas stations anyway, without electricity to pump it, so refilling before she left had not been an option. As she stepped out in the middle of the highway among several other abandoned cars, April knew she had to find a way to get some fast.

The three men that emerged from that house at the sound of her approach had other plans that didn't include helping her on her way, however. Cornered and alone on that deserted road, April was determined to fight to the death to deprive them of the one thing they wanted. The first to lay a hand on her paid with blood when the big folding knife she concealed in her back pocket found his throat. April used the moment of shock to try and run from the other two, but one was faster and she was thrown to the pavement and disarmed. She was certain she would have lost the fight if not for the surprise that came next in the form of deadly arrows from an unseen archer. Both men fell before they knew what hit them and April leapt to her feet to face the new threat. It was then that Mitch Henley showed himself, stepping out of the concealment of the roadside bushes and walking towards her with a reassuring wave, his bow arm relaxed at his side.

Thus began their brief but intense friendship, a bond strengthened by a long and difficult journey that involved more blood and death, but brought her at last to be reunited with her precious Kimberly. It had been a sad day when they parted outside the gates of a fortified church in Hattiesburg where David and his parents had taken Kimberly for refuge. But April had known all along Mitch wouldn't stay there and that she couldn't follow him—at least until all these months later, when life in that fortress became unbearable and too dangerous to remain.

Getting out of the city at last and finding her way back to Black Creek with Kimberly and David had been hard enough. And now, just when she'd thought the journey was almost over, April simply could not locate the obscure path to Mitch's land. It was incredibly frustrating, but there was nothing else to do but to camp for the night and keep searching in the morning.

All of them were tired, and Kimberly's needs had to be taken care of. David knew no more of camping and river travel than April did before the blackout, so she made the decision as to where they would land the canoe and where they would sleep for the night. She picked a high, narrow sandbar with a stand of tall hardwoods behind it, pulling the canoe well above the water's edge in case an upstream rain caused it to rise overnight. They would sleep on the open sand at the edge of the woods, because Mitch had told her

23

that the big diamondback rattlers that were common in these parts were nocturnal and on the prowl on the forest floor at night. April knew he said they sometimes ventured out on the sandbars too, but she felt better sleeping on the white sand that reflected the moonlight so well and at least made it possible to see a snake before stepping on it. She would have much preferred a tent with securely zippered doors, but they were lucky to even have blankets and those would have to suffice.

Four

"YOU AND STACY REALLY need to stay here, Lisa. Jason and I can handle this," Mitch said. "It was probably just one guy, and he has probably moved on by now anyway. But in case he hasn't or there are more of them, the two of us can move faster and quieter than four.

"But if there are more, you might wish you had our help, Mitch!" Lisa argued. "Why do we always get stuck staying here, guarding the house?"

"Because somebody has to, that's why. I could do this alone, but Jason is getting a lot better at tracking and stalking and this will be a good drill for him. You know we've got to be ready when these trespassers and poachers come around. We've been through all this before."

"Corey and Samantha can guard the house. It's not like they're doing anything else useful."

"Don't be so hard on them, Lisa. They've been through a lot. And you know as well as I do that we can't leave them here in charge of watching the place with everyone gone. They have no experience with guns or any other skills they would need for the job. You and Stacy do, Lisa. That's why I trust you with a responsibility that's just as important as what Jason and I have to do. Besides, we won't be gone long at all, and if we don't find whoever shot that arrow, all we're going to be doing is packing deer meat back home anyway."

Mitch finished his breakfast of fresh eggs and venison steak and stepped out into the cold of the morning. The pale edge of dawn was just beginning to push back the darkness that enveloped the Henley farm and the forest beyond. Jason was already outside, anxious to get started, armed with the Smith & Wesson AR-15 that was Doug Henley's state-issued patrol rifle. Mitch knew his dad would be glad they had the weapon, but he also knew that if he could, Doug Henley would much rather be here using it to watch over them himself.

Seven months had passed and every day Mitch had maintained hope that his mom and dad would arrive at the gate to the property, somehow making their way back to south Mississippi from Houston, Texas. But though he wouldn't let the hope die, Mitch couldn't deny the probability that his parents were no longer alive. For all he knew, they had died that first day of the blackout, victims of a plane crash caused by solar flare's powerful pulse. No one could have imagined the devastation wrought by this unseen force; planes falling from the sky…cars and trucks stalling on the highways and city streets…cell phones and lights shutting down for keeps…. The EMP destroyed practically everything electronic, and consequently, all systems dependent upon and controlled by computer and electrical circuitry.

Mitch didn't know if his parents' connecting flight from New Orleans had landed before it happened or not. If it didn't, his parents wouldn't have had a chance. Though he tried not to think about it too often, this seemed the most likely explanation as time went on. Doug Henley was as good a woodsman and as dedicated a lawman as any man could be. Mitch knew that if he were alive, his dad would do everything in his power to stay that way and keep his mom safe too. And Mitch knew that aside from that, he would make it his mission to get back home to him and his little sister. Nothing would stop him from doing so, but seven months was a long time, even without transportation and even with all the obstacles anyone on the move would surely encounter. If they were okay, Mitch was sure they would have arrived long before now.

But until they got here, if they ever did, keeping his sister safe and protecting the house and livestock from marauding looters was Mitch's responsibility. He was managing so far, but each new unknown, each new variable like this mysterious hunter who had wounded a deer so close to the house, was a potential threat to their safety that had to be investigated without delay.

With Jason carrying the AR-15, Mitch felt okay with his decision to stick to just his hunting bow as his main weapon. As he had proven more than once since law and order fell apart, the silence of his deadly arrows could offer great advantage in certain situations. But in case he got in a bind and needed a backup, he was also wearing his Ruger .357 Magnum revolver in a holster on his belt.

"I'm sure we'll be back in time for lunch," Mitch reassured his little sister as he kissed her on the cheek. Lisa was clearly unhappy that she couldn't participate in this patrol to find the trespasser. No doubt she saw it as an exciting break in the day-to-day monotony of living on the isolated farm with no outside contact, no communication and little entertainment besides what they created for themselves. Mitch knew it had to be incredibly boring for his fourteen-year-old sister, but he figured Lisa and her best friend Stacy were coping with it better than most.

For Mitch, there was nothing boring about it. Even before the blackout, there was nothing he would rather do than roam the woods alone with his bow and arrows. Now he was doing that everyday, and not for recreation or diversion but as a way of life. He had turned seventeen in the intervening months since everything changed, and he'd taken to this new life with great enthusiasm. If not for his worry and sadness over his parents' absence, Mitch could not have imagined a life he would enjoy more. For one thing, he no longer had to attend that hated school with its idiotic and petty rules and regulations. He didn't have to worry about fitting into a teenage social stratum that he neither cared about nor understood. He didn't have to live by clocks and bells, spend hours sitting on his butt at a stupid desk, or racking his brain trying to solve insanely complex algebra problems that he could see no use for in real life.

Mitch knew the electromagnetic pulse caused untold suffering and death, and undoubtedly affected millions of lives if not all the lives on the planet, but if nothing else good came of it, at least it had freed him from a way of life he never felt was right for him. Now he was living the fantasy he'd often entertained of going back in time—back to a time when all men lived by the weapons and the skills they carried with them when they set out each day into the forest to find what sustenance it provided. As always before a hunt, Mitch felt the tinge of excitement and anticipation as he strung his longbow and slung the deerskin quiver of cane-shafted arrows over his shoulder. As he strode across the yard with Jason close behind, he was eager to melt into the shadows of the trees where once again he would become that primal hunter he knew he was born to be.

Five

WHEN DARKNESS CLOSED IN on the small sandbar, the surrounding forest felt like solid walls closing cutting them off completely from the rest of the world. April knew it was an illusion though, and that even though it seemed impossible to leave their camp now even if they had to, Mitch had shown her otherwise. She had followed him through these same trackless woods on another night equally dark, amazed at how unerringly he found his way. And she'd seen how he used the darkness to his advantage to stalk and kill those who had taken his sister captive. Thinking of this, April couldn't help but feel vulnerable now, sitting there in the light of their campfire, just as those unsuspecting men had been doing before falling to Mitch's arrows. Was someone out there watching even now? She tried not to think about it, but found she couldn't help it. There were no human footprints or any other sign anyone had visited the sandbar recently; she had checked carefully for that as soon as they stopped. But she still couldn't get the idea she was being watched out of her mind. These deep woods were a scary place to be at night, even if it wasn't her first time. All she could do was hope the night passed quickly, knowing she would feel better at dawn. She *had* to find Mitch tomorrow, and she was determined to do so.

It was a mistake not to just get Kimberly and come back here with him in the first place after he helped her reach Hattiesburg. April knew this now. Mitch had, of course, invited all of them, including David's parents to come back with him, but though April saw the advantages of getting away from the city, the others did not. They were determined to remain in the big church sanctuary on Hardy Street, living off the provisions stored there that had been collected for a Central American relief mission before all this happened. The supplies would not last indefinitely, but it was enough to see the congregation through for several weeks, and few then could foresee the situation lasting longer than that. But it had lasted longer—much longer indeed—and there was still no end in sight.

April had asked Mitch and his sister to stay there with them too, but the city was no place for a guy like Mitch and she knew it. So they'd said their goodbyes and he and Lisa set out to return to the land he knew so well, where they would hold out and wait in hopes their parents were somehow still alive.

As April poked at the coals of the fire with a long stick, she thought about how glad she was to be away from those people in Hattiesburg, even though they were temporarily lost and alone in the woods. It had been tolerable there at first, but as time went by, she began to hate it in the confines of the church. A group of men including the pastor had taken charge with absolute authority, regimenting their days and restricting the activities of the members and other refugees to the tasks they assigned. And April and David, as unwed parents, were forced to go through the motions and exchange the vows of man and wife if they wanted to remain. She went along with it because she had no choice, but April considered the ceremony meaningless as there was no marriage license or legal recording of it a courthouse and she did not consider herself subject to the authority of a church she did not belong to. She'd once planned to marry David when she first found out she was pregnant, but that was before they started fighting and before she realized just how immature he really was. They were on the verge of splitting up most of the time they were living together in their New Orleans apartment and she had not been intimate with him since. During their time in Hattiesburg she poured all of her love and devotion onto Kimberly, only tolerating him because their daughter needed her father too.

What bothered April more than the forced marriage imposed upon them was the way the leaders turned away everyone who came to their doors begging for sanctuary or a meal to sustain them one more day. Any who approached were met by armed men, just as she and Mitch and Lisa had been challenged on that day they first arrived there. If not for David's parents and her baby already inside, she would have been denied as well. April knew that the supplies they had were limited, but there were some cases in which she felt an exception should be made. But all were turned away with equal disregard, and arguments among the members led to yet more rules and more power struggles within. April knew it was just human nature that the breakdown of one control structure would lead to the establishment of another. Most people seemed to thrive on it, but as non-members and outsiders accepted only because of David's parents, she and David had no say in anything. The two of them were given the most menial chores and expected to work long hours for their meals and protection within the church walls.

But even the protection was questionable. At first there were a few shootouts at the gate and incidents of unsuccessful nighttime raids by small, disorganized gangs. Then, towards the end of summer, there was a focused and coordinated attack by a gang of outlaws who rode into town on old Harley Davidson motorcycles, their machines unfazed by the pulse. The fighting had been intense, and more than a dozen of the defenders had died behind the barricade of trucks and SUVs encircling the grounds beyond the front door. Only the advantage of numbers, their fortified positions and sufficient firepower had enabled them to prevail against such a determined horde. April knew from what she'd seen outside with Mitch that more would come. This was just the beginning, and one day a stronger, even more dangerous group would arrive at the gates. Like Mitch said, there was no place in any city that was defensible indefinitely without outside help, of which they had still seen no sign. This most recent battle was a breaking point for April. She was determined to leave and get her baby to someplace that would not draw the attention of such organized attacks. And the only place she knew like that was far from cities and towns, deep in the woods in the river lands she had traveled with Mitch. There, his family property contained the shelter, tools, weapons, natural resources and most importantly, the isolation to ride out the aftermath of this crisis.

The act of leaving the barricaded church in Hattiesburg more resembled a prison escape than a decision they made with the blessing of the congregation. Once David had agreed to go with her, they began hoarding a small amount of their daily rations and secreting away other things they would need when the opportunity to get out presented itself. Though it had involved considerable risk, that opportunity came when the building was once again under attack. They were able to slip away in the confusion and noise after dark, carrying their weapons, a small amount of food, and their precious Kimberly hidden away in the blankets they were now using as bedding.

What little food they had brought was nearly gone, but April knew that once they were at Mitch's place starvation would be unlikely. And if necessary in the meantime, the Ruger carbine he'd given her before would provide a means of taking game. She didn't expect to have to resort to that yet, though. She was still confident that tomorrow they would find the path they sought. David, however, was far less certain, but to her relief, he sat sulking in silence and said no more about it.

They were both too tired from a long day of paddling to sit up half the night arguing. With Kimberly snuggled up next to her in the blankets, April fell fast asleep and didn't wake until the morning sunlight reached her face on the open sandbar. Sunny or not, the morning chill forced her to get up and stir the coals to rekindle last night's fire. A film of frost on the upturned hull of the canoe told her the low must have dropped to near freezing. It was the coldest night of the fall so far, and certainly the coldest since the blackout.

She was grateful that Kimberly was still asleep, and even more so that David had not yet stirred. She wanted to collect her thoughts as she built up the fire, and as she sat there poking at the coals with a stick and feeding more fuel into it, she tried harder to visualize exactly what the surroundings looked like that day she had followed Mitch on the obscure path from the creek to his family's home. With the flames blazing warm once again, she closed her eyes and tried to retrace her steps that day in her mind, looking for details that might make it more obvious later that morning as they resumed their search for the path. She knew it was close. It simply *had* to be.

The fire was crackling and sizzling now as the resin-rich driftwood burned hot. April snapped out of her meditation to move back a bit, and that's when she looked beyond the canoe, to the far end of the sandbar where it curved around the creek bend downstream. Standing there in plain view, all of them watching her intently were four men dressed in camouflage hunting clothing. All carried rifles except for one, who was armed with some kind of modern hunting bow quite different from the kind Mitch carried. April felt a surge of panic as she glanced from the armed strangers to David and Kimberly, still asleep in the blankets. And as she looked, her eyes fell upon the semi-automatic carbine that she now wished she had not foolishly left there, some ten or twelve feet away, hopelessly out of reach.

Six

MITCH HENLEY KNEW IT would be foolish and dangerous to dismiss the unknown archer as incompetent simply because he or she had made a poor shot and failed to follow up on tracking down the wounded deer. Any number of explanations could account for that, and he was aware as he set out with Jason that whoever it was might be back on the trail now, or worse, might have found the hanging and partially butchered carcass where he had left it. To avoid running into a surprise, Mitch planned to circle around and approach the ravine from the opposite direction.

He knew the drainage well, and once he and Jason reached it, Mitch communicated to him with hand signals as they stalked and stopped, and stalked and stopped, each time freezing for several moments to listen carefully before moving again. This tedious approach took nearly an hour, but it was worth it because once they reached the place where the deer was hanging, Mitch was certain no one was in the immediate vicinity. Ignoring the meat they would return for later, Mitch led the way across the ravine to the opposite side, where he once again picked up the blood trail that led him here the evening before. Following it back to where he'd first jumped the doe was relatively straightforward. Mitch remembered the spot and could have walked directly to it, but once again, he and Jason took the careful approach, stalking as they backtracked the deer's exact path to make sure no one else was following the sign from the opposite direction.

The real tracking work began when they reached the bloody spot where the doe had been laying up and would have probably bled out and died if Mitch had not come along and spooked it. From this point, Mitch intended to backtrack the scattered drops of blood to where the deer had first been hit. In doing so, he hoped to find footprints or some other clue to tell him who had fired that arrow and from where they had come. Jason was an eager apprentice to this business of hunting and tracking, but this was a trail far too important to risk eradicating any sign, no matter how small or seemingly insignificant. So Mitch made Jason stay behind him where he could not make a misstep, and each time he found new evidence of the fleeing deer's passing, he pointed it out both as part of his ongoing teaching and to warn him to stay clear.

They crept on this way for almost another hour, until the morning sun was high enough that its rays began to filter through the canopy of the trees and reach the forest floor in scattered spots. It was in this muted sunlight that Mitch at last found what he was looking for. In the middle of a sandy dry wash that wound through a stand of tall hardwoods, he saw the deep prints and disturbed sand where the deer's hooves had dug in as it made its first startled leap. Leading to this spot from the other side of the grove, a set of evenly spaced hoof prints clearly showed where the animal had been walking at a normal pace until its grazing was so rudely interrupted by an arrow strike. Remembering that he'd found the broken shaft buried in the deer's right flank, Mitch could be fairly certain of the angle from which the arrow had flown since he could see the direction the doe had been walking when she was hit. Considering the density of the grove of trees surrounding the sandy wash, he also knew that the archer could not have gotten a clear shot from that angle from more than thirty or forty yards away.

That there were no human footprints overlaying the deer's tracks in the area that it had been hit seemed strange. Why did the shooter not follow up to try and find his wounded game? Or, if he thought he'd missed the shot entirely, why did he not at least walk over to look for his arrow? Mitch wouldn't have been surprised at this kind of behavior before the blackout, but could anyone who'd survived this long in the aftermath really be that lazy when it came to hunting? He doubted it, figuring instead something else must have distracted him to cause him to give up the deer. Motioning for Jason to stay put, Mitch began a systematic search in the area he deduced was the most likely spot from which the arrow had flown. It only took a few minutes to prove his calculations correct. Next to the base of a giant white oak tree, the leaves littering the ground had been squashed into the soft mud by heavy, lugged soles, the kind commonly found on hiking or hunting boots. Mitch compared them to his own size eleven moccasins and judged them to be at least one size bigger, meaning the shooter was almost certainly an adult male. Though he looked for additional tracks and signs that the archer had a companion, there were none to be found. The boot prints led from the direction of the creek to the huge tree trunk, from behind which the man must have shot the deer and then turned back to retrace his steps to wherever he'd come from.

"Do you think he's still close by?" Jason whispered as he rejoined Mitch after being waved over.

"It's possible, but he hasn't been back here today. For some reason he just took the shot and turned around and went back the way he came."

"That's weird."

"Yeah, I could see this happening before, when people hunted for sport and killed animals for no reason, but it makes no sense now."

"So what do we do?"

"Follow him, of course, at least if there's a trail to be found. I want to know where he went and whether or not he was alone."

The problem was that following someone's trail through this environment was a challenge for any tracker. Mitch was good at it and getting better every day, but he knew he was still a long way from the realm of the real experts, like the

Apache scouts and mountain men of old he'd read so much about and tried so hard to emulate. The biggest obstacle was all the leaf litter that was several inches deep on the forest floor in most of the area. The few exceptions were places like the sandy wash and the clay and mud banks along the creek and its tributaries where heavy rains and flood waters occasionally swept the ground bare. Mitch knew he couldn't find all the tracks in between these scattered places, but from the few he did find, he could guess the path most people would take to get around thickets and other obstacles. Just like deer and other game, humans moving through the woods usually sought the path of least resistance and were fairly predictable if one knew what to look for.

One thing he was sure of, the tracks he could see led back in the direction of Black Creek. Whoever had made them had probably come into the area by following the waterway, either in a canoe or other small boat or by walking along the banks. The latter would be extremely difficult and slow. Mitch figured a canoe was more likely. So he and Jason would make their way to the banks where they could search the bare areas for more tracks or possibly the drag marks that would show where a canoe landed.

Before the electromagnetic pulse, Black Creek was a popular destination for weekend canoeists, especially in the summer months. And in the fall and winter, hunters sometimes used the waterway to access remote areas of the national forest lands that bordered much of the stream. As one of only two game wardens assigned to the county where their farm was located, Mitch's dad, Doug Henley, had arrested his share of poachers and other outlaws that operated on the creek out of small, outboard-powered Johnboats and the occasional motorized canoe. That was the main reason he was so careful to make sure there was no obvious path leading from the banks of the creek to their land, which at its nearest corner was less than a half a mile away. Now that most motor vehicles had been rendered inoperable, the creek was even more likely to be used by those traveling through the area, and Mitch had been patrolling its banks on a regular basis, keeping an eye on this backdoor entrance to their land while also watching the county road out front.

This was mainly because he knew that while most of the recreational paddlers who passed through the area only saw a small portion of the stream, Black Creek continued on much farther beyond the national forest area, merging eventually with the parallel stream, Red Creek, and then emptying in to the Pascagoula River. The total downstream distance from the area of their land to the urban centers of the Mississippi Gulf Coast was only a little over one hundred miles. Mitch knew that it was inevitable that some of the survivors from the heavily-populated coastal region seeking refuge in rural areas would make their way up the rivers and streams eventually. Black Creek was just one of many arteries that made up hundreds of miles of river lands in the Pascagoula

Basin. These streams would offer savvy survivors an isolated route to travel, as well as a source of water and plentiful game and fish along the way. It was something that was on his mind a lot as Mitch thought about how he would keep his little group safe as the weeks and months went by with still no relief in sight from the outside.

So far, if there had been anyone passing by on the creek by canoe or boat since Mitch and Lisa had returned to the farm from Hattiesburg, they did not stop. On the larger Leaf River, they had seen a few others with working outboard motors mounted on aluminum Johnboats. Most such motors in use on these rivers by fishermen before the blackout were the small and simple two-stroke variety with no electrical circuitry that could be affected by the pulse. It was less common to see outboards on Black Creek because of the wilderness designation and the numerous shoals and snags, but Mitch knew that was likely to change now, especially any regard for rules and regulations.

When he and Jason worked their way to within sight of the creek, Mitch headed straight for an area of clean-swept mud and found what he was looking for: the continuation of the hunter's trail. He only had to follow the clearly visible footprints a short distance to confirm his suspicions that the man who shot the deer was not alone. There, on the top of a small bluff overlooking the stream, the tracks merged with many others. It took Mitch a few minutes to sort them out by working his way up and down stream from where they joined, but at last he concluded there were four separate sets of footprints, including those of the mysterious bowhunter.

"I wonder how they got here?" Jason whispered.

"I'm betting by boat. These tracks are leading downstream. They could have come from downriver somewhere and may have a camp down there where they left their boat."

"Do you want to follow them?"

"Absolutely. We need to know, Jason. Maybe they've already left the area, but we have to try and find out."

The trail here was much easier to follow, as there were many patches of bare mud or sand along the banks where the four men couldn't have avoided leaving tracks even if they'd tried. It was obvious that they *hadn't* tried, probably because they thought they were totally alone in a really remote area and it didn't matter. Mitch was moving faster now, with Jason close behind, but he still wasn't taking unnecessary risks. At regular intervals he still stopped to look and listen, not wishing to suddenly run upon these men who were likely armed and who outnumbered him and Jason by two to one. It was during one of these deliberate stops that a sound far away in the forest reached his ears. At first, Mitch wasn't sure that it wasn't just the sound of the creek gurgling around some submerged tree or stump, but the more intently he listened, the more certain he was that what he was hearing was the sound of *voices*.

Seven

APRIL FOUGHT TO KEEP her voice steady and calm as she responded to the greeting of "good morning" from the first of the four men who strode across the sandbar. Not wanting to show concern and to appear calm, she remained seated by the campfire. Jason and Kimberly were still sleeping behind her, unaware of the unexpected visitors.

April tried to reassure herself that although she had been quite startled upon seeing strangers appear so suddenly out of nowhere, her surprise did not necessarily mean the four were up to no good. Maybe they were simply fellow survivors out hunting to support themselves and their families. It was likely they were just as surprised as she at encountering others in such a remote place.

"You sure didn't pick a very safe place to camp, out in the open like this," the same man who'd greeted her said as the four of them stopped a few paces away, on the opposite side of the smoky driftwood fire.

"We were only staying here long enough to sleep. We stopped for the night when it got too dark to paddle."

"So where are you going? There's nothing but woods

downstream for days."

As April considered how she would respond to this, she saw David stir out of the corner of her eye. He sat up with a start when he realized they were not alone. His eyes met hers and she hoped her expression conveyed that she was trying to remain calm despite the underlying fear she could not shake at being surprised this way first thing in the morning. David hadn't experienced nearly what she had since the pulse occurred. He had been in Hattiesburg the entire time, and though there had been attacks on the church, this was the first time since the event he had traveled without the protection of a large group. But April had already survived a few dangerous confrontations. With her determination and the skills she'd learned from her late father, not to mention Mitch Henley's help, she'd managed to prevail each time. She knew the reality of the dangers they faced in this lawless world, where anarchy and survival of the fittest now reigned. She could delude herself into believing these men had only innocent intentions, but hard experience had taught her not to take anything for granted. And if her distrust proved warranted, she didn't want them to know what she was capable of, either. The element of surprise had saved her before and it would be her best chance again, if it came to that.

But David had none of this experience or skill. Sure, he'd helped defend the church when the attacks from the outside came, but that was all long range stuff, shooting from behind the safety of a barricade at people who were too far away to even see the expressions on their faces. Here, the advantage of distance was already lost. The four strangers were upon them and her rifle was out of reach.

"This is my husband," April said when the one doing the talking gave her a questioning look upon David's awakening.

David got to his feet, picking up a drowsy Kimberly as he did, and extending his hand to introduce himself. "I'm David Greene. This is my wife, April, and our daughter, Kimberly."

The man nodded but did not except David's offered hand. When he didn't, David began apologizing. "Look, if we're trespassing on your land, we're sorry. We just stopped for the night to get some rest. We thought this was national forest land."

The man just chuckled a bit to himself and turned to grin at his companions, who were also smiling. He raised one arm and turned first one way and then the other, taking in the surroundings in a sweeping gesture meant to indicate everything in sight was included in his next comment. "The old boundaries are no more, David. Who can say who owns this land when there is no one here to claim it but us? The forest service and the government are abstract entities, and at best, absentee owners. For all we know, they do not even exist in the way that they once did. The lines are being redrawn and old designations and names mean nothing. This *is* our land at the moment because this is where we are, but I'm not questioning your right to camp here. I'm just naturally curious and wanted to know where you're going and where you came from. It's dangerous to travel at all these days, and even more so with a woman and a small child."

"We're going to...."

"We came from Hattiesburg," April answered for him. "And we're not alone. We are with a group of people from my husband's church. They are in several canoes but some pushed on ahead of us last night and will wait for us until we catch up this morning. The others are somewhere upstream; behind us. We are going to a youth camp the church owns that is right on the banks of the creek, in the next county downstream. The whole congregation is going there, because staying in the city is no longer safe."

The stranger asking the questions looked at his companions with a confused expression. "I didn't see a church camp downriver, did any of you? I can't recall passing any other canoes on the river, either."

The man nearest him, who was carrying a short semiautomatic rifle that April now knew was some variety of an AR-15, was the first to answer. "Nope, I haven't seen a soul out here, Wayne."

The other two shook their heads in agreement. Now all of them had their gaze fixed on April to see what she would say next. But David spoke again instead.

"We're just trying to get our daughter to safety, that's all. You can imagine how difficult it is to know where to go."

"How old is she?" the one the other had called Wayne

asked.

"She's nearly two," April answered, as she began backing away from the men across the sand, in a move to get closer to David and take Kimberly into her own arms.

"Wait!" Wayne stopped her. "Don't move any closer to that rifle!"

April froze as the other man with AR leveled his weapon at her. One of the other two stepped forward at a nod from the leader and moved to pick up April's carbine from where it was laying on her blanket, next to the longbow Mitch had given her.

"I just wanted my baby! DON'T YOU TOUCH HER!" April screamed, looking at the one who was now holding her gun and her bow.

"We don't want anything to do with your kid," Wayne said. "I just didn't want you to get any ideas about doing something funny with that weapon. A man can't be too careful around strangers these days."

"*You* are the ones who came uninvited into our camp brandishing weapons," April replied. "I'm not dumb enough to try something stupid like that with the four of you standing there with guns in your hands. I just don't want you frightening my child!"

When the other man had reached for the carbine, David had stepped back out of the way with Kimberly putting her even farther out of reach. April knew there was another rifle under his blanket, a bolt-action Winchester .270 that had been issued to him by the church members for his duty as a defender, but with their child in his arms she knew he wouldn't make a foolish move for it. She was glad that it was out of sight, but it was useless to them now whether the men saw it or not. What could either of them do with one bolt-action rifle against three men armed with semiautomatics who were standing over them at the ready? And although the talkative one, the one called Wayne, carried that weird, high-tech bow instead of a rifle, he was also wearing a Glock in a low-slung holster strapped to his thigh.

"Ruger Mini-14," the one who had picked up the gun said as he held it up for the others to see.

This elicited another chuckle from the rest of the men. "Piece of worthless junk for hunting," Wayne said. "You probably couldn't hit a deer broadside with that thing at eighty yards."

April knew better but said nothing. The rifle had already accounted for more than one man who'd decided to use the circumstances as an excuse to revert to indecency and savagery.

"I don't know what the hell this stick is for," the other man said, holding up her bow in his other hand.

"Why that's a homemade longbow, Jared. It's just not strung. So, who's the archer?" Wayne turned to David. "Is that your stick bow?" He had an even bigger grin on his face as he viewed the simple wooden weapon with obvious contempt. From the machine-like contraption he carried,

April knew he wouldn't appreciate the careful craftsmanship Mitch had put into making the traditional weapon he loved so much. She didn't care what this jerk thought though, really.

"I am," she said.

"Really? Can you hit anything with it? I'd like to see that!"

"I don't have any arrows left. But look, we were just getting ready to pack up and leave. We've got a long way to go today and we need to get on the river early. If you don't trust me with my carbine, then just unload it and give it back to me. We'll just paddle away and you'll never see us again. But we really need to get going."

"It didn't look like you were in a hurry to me," Wayne said, glancing up at the sun. "It must be nearly nine o'clock by now. Your husband and the baby girl were still sacked out and you were just rekindling the fire. You can't tell me you weren't going to have some breakfast first, and probably coffee to go with it, especially on a crisp morning like this. I'll bet you've got coffee in your bags there, haven't you? We haven't had our coffee this morning. In fact we haven't had any coffee in so long I can barely remember what it tastes like. Why don't you put some water on to boil and let's all sit down and visit over a cup or two?"

"We don't *have* coffee! Really, I'm telling you the truth. We barely got out of Hattiesburg with enough food for just a few days. Wherever you guys have come from, you know as well as I do how scarce things like coffee are by now. It's hard enough just getting something to eat."

"I'm sure it is, with that crappy Mini 14 with iron sights and a homemade bow; not to mention a lazy husband that sleeps past sunup!"

"Hey! I'm not lazy!" David said, a touch of anger in his voice. "We paddled all day yesterday. We didn't get any sleep the two nights before. I was just catching up a bit."

Wayne just shook his head and looked at April again with that grin that was totally dismissive of anything David had to say. She was getting really creeped out by this guy and what she wanted more than anything was for him and his friends to just *leave*. But she already knew that wasn't going to happen, at least not as quickly and painlessly as she wanted it to. What *was* happening was that a highly uncomfortable situation was developing, and it was shaping up to be a problem that would soon be out of control. Wayne and his friends weren't leaving until they got what they wanted, and April was beginning to realize that what they wanted might just be *her*.

Eight

THE VOICES MITCH HEARD were too far away for him to understand any of what was being said, but as he stood motionless listening, he had no doubt that they were real and not some trick of gurgling water in the nearby creek. From Jason's expression, Mitch knew he could hear them too. Mitch didn't want to make a move though until he knew if the speakers were stationary, coming closer or moving farther away. As he listened he could pick out several distinct tones that told him the conversation was an exchange between more than just two people, and that at least one of them was a female. That was odd, because all of the four sets of tracks he'd been following since finding the place where the unknown archer had rejoined his companions were made by man-sized boots.

The voices were clearly coming from the direction in which the tracks led, so Mitch felt it safe to assume that at least some of those he could hear speaking were the same who had passed this way in company with the archer. If that were the case, they hadn't traveled far since wounding the deer late yesterday. The only explanation for that was that they must have camped nearby and perhaps even now were still at their campsite. Mitch wanted to know for sure, and to do that, he had to get closer, but Jason was a liability for that kind of reconnaissance. Although he was an eager student and Mitch had been patiently teaching him ever since he'd recovered from the brutal beating he'd received from the Wallace brothers who had kidnapped their little sisters, Jason still had a lot to learn. The art of stalking, in particular, was something Mitch had been perfecting since he was six or seven, when he first began pretending he was an Indian while playing games in which he tried to sneak up on his father in the woods and around their farm. He had practiced those skills from the time he began hunting with BB guns until he graduated to real firearms, and ultimately, the traditional bow and arrows he now favored above all else. It would be impossible for Jason or anyone else just starting out to approach anything near Mitch's level of competence in a few short months.

Realizing this, and considering the potential dangers of the situation, Mitch wasn't taking any chances on Jason making a misstep or otherwise alerting these strangers to their presence. It simply wasn't worth the risk. Stepping close to his friend so he could whisper into his ear, Mitch told him of his intentions and then led Jason to a hideaway in a bay thicket between the creek and the trail the men had made yesterday. Giving him instructions to stay put and keep a sharp lookout unless called, Mitch then slipped off into the direction of the voices, a broadhead arrow nocked and ready on his bowstring.

Mitch had no intention of confronting the trespassers, and certainly hoped he wouldn't need the arrow or the handgun strapped to his side. Ideally, he would observe them without being seen and hopefully ascertain that they were just passing through the area on their way to someplace else. Once he knew they were moving on, he could forget the incident and he and Jason would pack the remainder of the venison back to the house.

With Jason waiting behind, Mitch could move fast while still making little discernible sound. The key to moving quietly through the woods—he'd discovered through trial and error and diligent practice—was learning to scan the way ahead each time he stopped to look and listen. Doing this, he could pick in advance the best route for the next twenty or so steps, avoiding the worst patches of crackly, dry leaves, fallen branches and other obstacles to stealthy movement. Mitch did this instinctively now with little thought, weaving silently among the thickets and around trees in the path of least resistance as effortlessly as a city-bred pedestrian navigated busy streets and avoided getting hit by cars.

He was quickly out of Jason's view in a few moments, melting into the greenery in his head-to-toe camouflage. Mitch knew that whenever he paused to look and listen it was impossible for anyone to see him at a distance beyond a few yards. The form-breaking effect of the tree bark and leaf pattern camo was quite effective. Movement and only movement would allow him to be seen by either humans or wildlife, and so each time before moving again he carefully scanned his surroundings to make certain he was still alone. And when he did move, it was deliberate and fluid, with none of the quick or jerky patterns of the inexperienced and impatient that would announce his presence to every living thing within a hundred yards.

As he closed the distance to the source of the voices, it became apparent that the speakers were stationary rather than approaching or moving farther away. This was good news to Mitch, as it meant he could approach them on his own terms, getting as close as needed to observe them and establish their intentions. Each time he stopped to listen, a little closer than the last time, the individual voices became more distinct and he could begin to make out a few words. It was then that he realized this was not a normal conversation among friends. He could hear the tension in the voices as he listened, especially that of the woman or girl. He also heard for the first time the crying of a small child, as well as at least two or three distinct male voices. But he was still too far away to make out enough of it to figure out what the commotion was about. There was anger and fear in the exchange, of that he was certain, and the way it seemed to be escalating prompted Mitch to move as fast as he could while remaining stealthy. Something intense was happening, and though it wasn't his concern, he couldn't help his natural curiosity to find out what this was about.

In recent weeks survival on the Henley property had settled pretty much into an easy routine. It had been awhile since there had been any drama of any kind, much less real danger. Now all of a sudden with the discovery of the wounded deer, it seemed a lot was happening all at once. Even if the argument was a squabble over something that was none of his business, Mitch found it an interesting game to stalk closer and observe. Like when he was a kid playing such games every day, this was grand entertainment in a world where such diversions were few and far between.

The sounds of the voices were leading him along the creek bank now, and as he got closer, he became quite certain that whoever these people were, they were on the sandbar on the opposite bank from him. It was a sandbar he knew well, since it was so close to the house and this part of the creek was his extended backyard. He was glad of this really, because it meant they were out in the open where he could easily see them, but the bank on his side was heavily wooded and would make it easy for him to stay hidden.

It was only one more bend in the stream before the sandbar would be in view, so Mitch kept his approach slow but stopped less frequently now that he knew for sure where they were. Before he reached the beginning of the bend, he walked right into an area where the strangers had obviously camped for the night. That seemed odd, since he'd assumed they must have camped on the sandbar, since they were there now, this early in the morning. But the cleared away vines and other undergrowth, as well as the compressed leaves and scattered trash, left no doubt someone had slept here. Mitch picked up a torn MRE wrapper. There were three more on the ground nearby. Whoever these hunters were, they apparently still had supplies from before the collapse. Maybe that was why they hadn't bothered to try and track the deer, or maybe they were simply unskilled at hunting and were still living off stockpiles of survival food such as this. Mitch figured that was it, especially considering all the noise they were making now. Anyone with survival knowledge and experience would keep their voices lower, even if they *were* arguing and fighting. But even so, Mitch wasn't about to take it for granted that they were completely unaware or stupid. He left the campsite with as much caution as before as he neared the sandbar. He hadn't gone ten yards when he was stopped in his tracks by a scream from the woman he'd heard mixed in with the other voices. This time he could understand clearly what she said:

"DON'T YOU TOUCH HER!"

He heard the baby crying too, as well as the laughter of several men. Mitch began to wonder if what was going on was more than a simple domestic squabble. He'd followed the tracks of four men who'd clearly slept on this side of the creek that night, but now there was a woman who sounded sincerely distressed on the other side. Could she be another traveler not connected to these men at all and now the victim of a random attack? If so, it sounded like it was escalating even now. Mitch worked his way through the undergrowth as fast as he could without making noise, keeping his bow with the already-nocked broadhead low and to the front and ready as he moved.

When he at last reached the area adjacent to the downstream end of sandbar on the other side, he saw a single aluminum canoe pulled up on the sand, a line from the bow tying it to stump. The lettering on the bow identified the canoe as one that had belonged to the rental fleet in the town of Brooklyn, twenty miles upstream. Mitch figured most of the boats there had been taken by now, stolen by refugees desperate to get away from the dangers of the highways and roads. Few people could survive long out here in the wilds without supplies though, and if they kept going far enough downstream they would end up in a even more desperate situation on the urbanized Gulf coast. It didn't make sense that the four he'd been tracking were connected to the canoe, however, unless there was another one tied up around the bend upstream. These seventeen-foot Grummans were designed for two paddlers; three adults could fit in a pinch, but not four men.

The exchange seemed to become more heated as Mitch crept farther upstream, staying low in the cover of the undergrowth until at last he could see what was going on. There were four armed men with their backs to him, forming a rough semi-circle on his side of a smoldering campfire in the sand. Facing them from the other side of the fire were three people—a man, a woman and a small toddler that the man was holding in his arms. It was they who likely paddled the canoe here, Mitch surmised. And it was now clear the arguing he'd heard was a confrontation between the four he'd been tracking and these other strangers who must have spent the night there on the sandbar.

Mitch watched and listened; hoping to hear enough to determine exactly what was going on. It was not until the woman lunged to try and reach the child that Mitch got a clear view of her face. When he did, he felt a rush of adrenaline wash over him as he tensed and squeezed his hunting bow in a white-knuckle grip. How and why she was here he had no idea, but right there before his eyes, was someone he never expected to see again: *April Gibbs*!

Nine

APRIL'S MIND WAS RACING as she played out various scenarios of what might happen next and what she and David might do when it did. With her carbine already in their hands and the .270 out of reach under David's blanket, April was effectively unarmed but for her knife. Though she'd used it to great effect that first week of the blackout, this was a far different situation. For one thing, Kimberly was with her this time and equally in danger. For another, there were four of these men and they were all armed, not to mention no doubt hardened by the trials of survival as anyone who'd lived this long since the blackout must be. While she wouldn't hesitate to use the Spyderco as a last resort, and would make anyone who attacked her and Kimberly pay in blood, she doubted she and David had much of a chance if it came to an all-out assault from four men. What she hoped she could do was diffuse the situation and somehow get the men to go away.

"Look, I'm really sorry we don't have any coffee. If we did, I'd be glad to share some with you. But we don't have much of anything."

"We'll see," Wayne said. "Gary, see what's in those packs!

63

And check the blankets too."

"You don't have any right to go through our belongings!" April said, trying to hide her apprehension, as she now knew for sure they weren't going to simply go away. At the very least they would take what little rice and other staples she and David had, and she knew they were going to discover the other rifle too and would certainly take that as well. Without it or her carbine and bow, she and David would have nothing with which to defend Kimberly or hunt for food, even if the men did nothing else to harm them.

"Our *right* is the right of survival," Wayne said. "In case you haven't heard of it, there's this concept called 'survival of the fittest.' That means whoever is bigger, badder or has the most guns wins. It's the law of the jungle, sweetheart, and we're *in* the jungle now!"

"We don't have anything worth taking," David said. "We're just barely getting by, and what little we have isn't worth your time to bother with."

Wayne just looked at him with a smirk on his face and then turned to stare April up and down in a way that David could not misinterpret. "Oh I think it's worth my time all right! It must have been worth yours too, considering that rug rat you're holding."

April lunged to grab Kimberly from David, but Wayne quickly stepped between them, cutting her off. At the same time, the one searching their belongings, the one he'd called Gary, found the hunting rifle and held it up for the others to see. When David tried to move around Wayne to get to April's side, Gary jabbed the butt of the rifle into his stomach, doubling him over, and barely missing Kimberly, who he was holding against his chest. Before David could catch his breath and straighten up, Gary swung the stock up in a swift uppercut motion that connected to the side of his head, causing him to collapse into the sand, dropping Kimberly as he fell. The child cried out in terror as April screamed and tried again to lunge for her. But Wayne knocked her aside with a backhand slap, sending her to her hands and knees in the sand. At the same time, Gary snatched Kimberly up and began backing away with her in his arms.

At the sight of her child being grabbed, the animal instinct took over and April was transformed the savagery of a lioness defending her cub. Her martial arts training and fighting instinct kicked in and she no longer cared that she was unarmed and outnumbered. She shook off the blow and leapt to her feet, quickly buckling Wayne's knee with a sweep kick, following it up with a palm heel strike to the nose while he was still unbalanced. The big man fell with blood pouring over his thick mustache. April didn't wait to see what would happen next before she whipped out the Spyderco folder she carried in her back pocket, snapping the blade open and locked with a lighting-fast, one-hand motion. It was a futile gesture though, as the other two men advance with their rifles pointed straight at her and Gary yelled to get her attention.

He was brandishing a drawn blade of his own, a big flashy Bowie knife, the edge poised just inches from Kimberly's delicate throat. April knew they had her at that point. If she continued the attack, she would either be shot or Kimberly would be killed. And David could do nothing for her now, sprawled, as he was, unmoving and unconscious in the sand. April lowered her hand and let the Spyderco fall from her open fingers.

"You don't have to hurt my daughter. You can have whatever you want. Just please! Get that knife away from her. She's just a baby! Please!"

Wayne was getting up now, brushing the sand off his pants and holding a bandana against his bloody nose. At the sight of this, the other two men with the rifles couldn't suppress a chuckle and Gary grinned too as he lowered his big Bowie away from Kimberly but kept it in his hand, unsheathed and ready.

"Where in the hell did you learn how to do that?" Wayne asked as he appraised her again from head to toe. "I've got to say, I'm impressed. And the way you whipped out that blade. Crap! You could've *cut* somebody!"

"It wouldn't have been the first time!" April said, as she stepped back and allowed him to reach down and pick up the knife her father had given her all those years ago, shortly before he passed away.

"I can believe that. But you won't get a chance to try it again! At least not if you care what happens to that little girl of yours."

"What do you want from us? Just give her back to me and leave us *alone!*"

"That would be crazy. You'd never last out here alone and unarmed. Though you might as well have been alone for all *he* could have done to help you." Wayne nodded in the direction of David's limp figure, collapsed in the sand.

April didn't think David was dead, but the blow from the rifle stock had rendered him unconscious and he wasn't showing any sign of coming to.

"You didn't have to hit him like that," she glared at Rick. He was unarmed and he was just trying to protect our daughter. You could have killed him! Now give her back to me!"

Wayne looked at Gary and told him to put his knife away.

"Why do we need the rug rat?" he asked.

"Because her tough little momma here won't be trying anything stupid as long as she's got her arms full, that's why."

"You don't plan on bringing her with us, do you?" one of the other men asked. "I thought we would take our turns and be done right here. We don't need another mouth to feed—especially not two more!"

"He's right," Gary said. "How are we going to take care of a baby anyway?"

"We won't! That's her job. But she's going with us and the rest of you can keep your hands off!" Wayne said, as he wiped more blood from his bleeding nose. "This is between me and her now and she's got some making up to do before I'm done with her!"

"Just give me my baby!" April pleaded, as Kimberly continued to cry in terror in Rick's rough grasp. April tried to push past Wayne again to reach her, but he threw her roughly to the sand when she did. She landed near David's still body and attempted to crawl to his side to see if he was still breathing. Wayne stepped into her path and cut her off.

"Will you just let me check his pulse? We've got to do something for him. I'll go wherever you want me to if you don't hurt Kimberly, but we can't just leave her father here like this!"

"Of course we can and of course we will! If I didn't think he was so worthless at taking care of himself, never mind you and the baby, I'd put a bullet in his head right now. But if he does wake up before the coyotes and wild dogs find him, I want him to sit here and wonder why he didn't do a better job of learning how to be a man back when he had the chance. What did he do back in the world anyway, sit around all day and play video games while you went to work?"

This wasn't far from the truth, but April said nothing. There was nothing she could do for David now and no use pushing the subject. She wanted to ask Wayne why they were doing this to them. She wanted to ask them all who they were and what kind of people they were to treat others this way. But she said nothing because she already knew. They weren't people at all. The were simply animals—animals acting on their most instinctive and savage desires—exerting their dominance because in the absence of law and authority, they could do so with their superior numbers and weapons. She and David and Kimberly were simply in the wrong place at the wrong time when they woke that morning on the banks of Black Creek. Maybe David would come to on his own, and maybe he would find some way to survive. She doubted it, but whatever happened to him was beyond her control at this point. She had to focus on staying alive so she could take care of her baby. She knew the only way she could do that was to comply with these brutal men, and she was all too aware of what that would entail. She rose to her feet and faced Wayne and Gary once again, calmly asking for her child and letting them know she would resist no further.

Ten

MITCH WAS HOLDING HIS bow at full draw, but didn't even remember pulling it back, so automatic and unconscious was the motion. Each second that he held his right hand anchored to the right corner of his mouth, he could have relaxed the tips of the three fingers hooking the bowstring. All the energy stored in those perfectly balanced limbs of carved Osage orange would send the deadly broadhead-tipped arrow on its way with barely a whisper. Mitch knew he could easily put it through the neck or center mass of any of the four aggressors on the opposite side of the creek, and yet, he didn't.

Once he recognized April, he quickly realized the man with her was David, the father of her child. He'd only met the guy once, and little Kimberly, of course, at her age looked much different after seven months than she did the one and only time he had seen her as well. How and why the three of them came to be here on this Black Creek sandbar so close to home was beyond his comprehension at the moment and there was no time to ponder it. Unfolding before him was a fast-changing and unpredictable scene that put him in a real dilemma. When the larger man stepped between April and her little girl, David had tried to intervene, only to be struck to the ground by a rifle butt. Then the bigger man had backhanded April and knocked her down as well when she tried to get to Kimberly. Mitch could have let fly his arrow then and there and killed the man easily, and it was all he could do to restrain himself. But this situation was far too volatile. He had the element of surprise in his favor, and he was certain he could nock a second arrow and take out one more before they realized what was happening, but that would still leave two. Considering that all four of them were armed and pretty much surrounding April with weapons already on her, the odds were too high that something would happen to either her or little Kimberly before he could deal with them all. Mitch cursed his decision to leave his father's AR-15 with Jason. If he had the firepower of a semiautomatic rifle combined with a surprise ambush out of nowhere, it might be feasible to take care of this problem then and there. But wishing for something wouldn't make it happen, and all he could do was watch and wait for a better opportunity. He relaxed to half-draw to save his muscles from fatigue, but he was still ready to take the risk of shooting any second if there was no other way.

When April got back to her feet and put the man who'd hit her on the ground with a sweep kick and punch, drawing her knife when he fell, Mitch took aim again, certain he would have no choice but to intervene quickly. But the fight was over as soon as it started when one of the others grabbed

72

Kimberly and put a blade of his own to her throat. April had no choice but to drop her weapon, and Mitch was relieved he didn't have to shoot just yet. With two rifles aimed at her at point-blank range, and Kimberly's throat exposed to a knife, there was little Mitch could do at the moment that wouldn't make things worse. The best he could hope for was that April could buy some time without either of them getting hurt, giving him time to figure out a safer way to extract her and Kimberly from this mess.

He noted that David was still sprawled unmoving on the sand, and wondered if he was dead. The blow from the rifle stock struck his skull hard enough that Mitch had heard it clearly, even from the sixty-odd yards to his side of the creek. Dead or not, he was certainly out of commission. Whatever happened next was largely up to the four men and how April handled herself. Mitch knew she was smart enough to know her limits, he just hoped the men wouldn't try to do anything to her out in the open right then and there. He had no doubt of their intentions though; it was just a matter of when and where.

Watching what happened next, he could tell that the big man; the one she'd swept to the ground and pulled her knife on, was surprised and impressed with her abilities. The other men shared a good-natured chuckle at his expense, but not in a mocking kind of way. Mitch could tell they respected him and he figured they were probably all good friends; maybe this guy was just a bit older and they looked to him as a leader or something. Mitch saw the compound bow that he'd laid down when he confronted April, and seeing it, he knew this was the man who had wounded the small doe. Putting together the story that the trail he'd followed told, he figured it must have been a coincidence that they stopped to camp on his side of the creek while April, David and Kimberly unfortunately chose this particular adjacent sandbar the same evening. Mitch didn't know who arrived first, but he figured the men must have seen them the evening before and stayed out of sight until morning. That was probably why he found no evidence of a fire where they camped. He figured they waited until daylight, and then crossed the creek in an area of shoals just downstream and out of sight. April and David probably never saw them until they were upon them. These details mattered little anyway at this point. What was important was that he was here now and his presence was still unknown to any of them. He would find a way to do something, but he had to make sure he didn't make a mistake when it was time to act because there would only be one chance.

At least the tension was diffused somewhat after April dropped her knife. The one who had been holding Kimberly put her down at the other's request, and April swept the child up in her arms. Mitch couldn't hear all of the conversation that ensued, but at one point he heard April asking to be allowed to check on David and he heard the man's refusal to let her do so. He heard the man say that they were going to leave him for dead, whether he was or not. The others were going through the scattered belongings where the three had slept and Mitch gathered they were getting ready to leave, taking April and Kimberly with them. It was what he expected they would do since they apparently weren't going to do anything to her here, and he was relieved because it would buy him a bit more time. That they were also taking Kimberly likely meant they intended to keep them both alive, at least for the immediate future.

Mitch had a tough decision to make. Jason was waiting back there barely within earshot of this spot and unaware of what exactly was happening. Mitch could forget about him and immediately follow wherever these four took April and Kimberly, but he knew it might take hours of trailing them before he found the right opportunity for a rescue that did not involve too much risk. On the other hand, if he had that rifle Jason was carrying, the odds would be much more in his favor, even if he used the bow to silently take out the first one or two. Besides that, if he just disappeared now, taking no telling how long to follow until the right moment presented itself, Jason would have no way of knowing what happened. Even if he somehow managed to follow the tracks the rest of the way here, he would arrive only to find an abandoned canoe and a dead or unconscious stranger lying on the sandbar. He wouldn't know what to make of it, and not knowing what happened to his friend, he would probably go back to the house and tell the others. Then Lisa and everyone else would be worried and upset and likely come looking for him. There were a lot of complications with that scenario.

Besides, if David *was* still alive, he was going to need help when he came to. Mitch decided the best thing he could do was wait until the men left, to make sure they did indeed set out to wherever they were going with April and Kimberly, then he would get back to Jason as fast as possible. He could easily pick up the trail when the two of them returned, as the four hunters would probably be just as careless today as they were the day before. After all, they had no reason to suspect anyone knew of their presence here or what they'd just done. He knew they would be leaving on foot, as the one canoe would be useless to a party that size. When Mitch returned with Jason, the two of them could use it to move David to this side of the creek, the side the farmhouse was on, if he was still alive. Then Mitch would take the rifle and set out in pursuit. Jason could go back to get help for David if he was still unconscious and unable to move on his own. Even if not for the matter of helping David, Mitch wouldn't take Jason with him because what he had to do required ultimate stealth.

Letting these men disappear from his sight with April and Kimberly as captives was the hardest thing Mitch had done in a long time. Even after thinking his plan through and knowing he was doing the logical thing, it was oh so hard to overcome his urge to use his arrows now, or at least stay close enough behind them to see their every move. He saw the one who'd held the knife to Kimberly's throat take a length of rope out of his hunting pack and fashion one end into a loop. Then, he saw the leader take the rope and affix the loop around April's neck like a leash, which he let out some six feet or so, wrapping the other end in his free hand to keep her close behind him. April was carrying Kimberly in her arms, the child hugging her close and no doubt terrified after all this yelling and fighting and seeing her daddy fall and not get back up. Mitch was glad that at least they were letting April carry her, but he wondered how long she could hold up doing so, especially in these dense and trackless woods that required ducking and weaving and negotiating mud and other tricky terrain.

The other men were carrying their rifles and packs as well as what they had taken from April and David's belongings in the camp. Mitch recognized the Ruger Mini 14 and the bow he'd given April all those months ago, and he also noted there was a bolt-action rifle they must have brought with them from the church, if that's where they came from. He wondered what could have happened to have caused April to come back here, to Black Creek, but he figured whatever it was, she must have come here looking for him, hoping to bring her family to the sanctuary of the Henley farm. Mitch was determined that she would get there too, whatever he had to do. He watched until they melted out of sight among the trees, heading in a downstream direction, then he turned and ran as quietly and swiftly as he could back to where Jason

INTO THE RIVER LANDS

waited.

Eleven

WAYNE PARKER COULDN'T REMEMBER the last time he'd had such a lucky day. Sure, there had been a few in the last seven months that weren't as bad as most, but this was a real *score*. This was like walking into the Beau Rivage casino back before the collapse and winning a grand on one pull at the five-dollar slots. But it was better than that, because there wasn't much you could do these days with money, whether it was ten dollars, a thousand dollars or a million. But a girl like this? That was something worth finding! Too bad the other guys thought it was their lucky day too. Wayne had put them off for now, convincing them they needed to move out without delay, but the issue would come up again, he knew this all too well. He would deal with it when it did.

He adjusted the noose of braided nylon rope around the girl's neck so that it was just snug enough to be persuasive, but not enough to cause pain or restrict her air flow. He wasn't worried about her trying to run. She couldn't as long as she had that little girl in her arms, and he knew there was no way she would run off and leave her. That was clear from the way she fought; as mean as a mama bear protecting her cubs. But nevertheless, Wayne wanted to know she was right behind him, following every step he took, and the rope would reassure him of that.

"So, that sorry excuse for a husband of yours said your name was April," he said as he looked directly into her eyes, his hands still on the noose, as he let the backs of his fingers rest on the soft skin of her neck. "I like that. I think it suits you; all fresh like spring. And Kimberly, your little girl; that's a nice name too."

When she said nothing, Wayne continued....

"I know you don't want to talk to me right now, but that'll change. We've got all the time in the world, but I don't think it'll take you long to realize how much better off you and your daughter are now. You're both safe with me. Nothing's going to happen to you as long as I'm around."

"Nothing would happen to us if you would just leave me and my child here. I can take care of myself without any help. I don't *want* any help!"

"Maybe. But maybe not. That was pretty impressive, the way you caught me by surprise. I didn't expect you to be carrying that blade either. I'll look forward to hearing where you learned to move like that. I haven't met many women who could have done that; really not any...."

When April didn't reply, Wayne carried on:

"I don't know where the three of you came from or where you thought you were going, but if you've survived this long since the blackout, you've got to know how dangerous it is everywhere. Anyone that's going to stay alive now has got to play it smart, and the smart ones have got to stick together. We know what we're doing and we've made it fine this far. You'll see when you meet the rest of our little tribe and realize how well prepared we are. It's not like some of us didn't see something like this coming for a long time before it did."

Wayne Parker had been expecting America to collapse any day for at least the last seven or eight years. He didn't see how things could possibly keep going the way they were with the state of the economy and the way people seemed so divided on every issue. He had grown up in Jackson County, the home of Ingalls Shipbuilding and much of the other heavy industry of Mississippi's Gulf Coast. Thirty-two years old when the lights went out, Wayne had worked in the oilfields off Louisiana since he'd graduated high school and then completed an underwater welding course shortly thereafter. He had made good money out on the rigs, working mostly two weeks on and two weeks off, but his ex-wife had taken most of it and the child support for his two sons that came out of his checks left him little better off than when he was single in his early twenties. But at least the bitter divorce cured him of any romantic notions he had entertained before about marriage. What was left after the child support payments, taxes and bills, he spent on temporary girlfriends, deer hunting and fishing boats.

Of those three, it was the deer hunting he loved the most.

INTO THE RIVER LANDS

He couldn't get enough of it and eventually he put all the extra money he could spare into buying some land with a few other guys he knew from work. The property was up in George County, less than an hour's drive from the rental house in Moss Point where he was living with his girlfriend, Tracy when the pulse hit. Whenever he was in from his hitch, especially if it was deer season, he practically lived at the cabin he and the guys had built there. The property they purchased together totaled nearly 200 acres, and it joined up to the tens of thousands more of federal and state public lands, most of it part of Desoto National Forest and a state wildlife management area. All in all, it was a vast expanse of river bottom forest, swamp and bayous and was virtually a wilderness once you got away from the few roads that skirted the edges.

When Wayne was out there with his friends, surrounded by woods in every direction, thoughts of his job, and the traffic and congestion of the coast far behind, he felt more alive than anywhere else. Things had changed a hell of a lot on the coast since he was a kid growing up there. For one, the legalization of gambling and the consequential growth in the form of casinos, hotels and housing for the influx of people to the area transformed the sleepy fishing towns he remembered into bustling resorts. People moved in from everywhere, many of them from up north and other places far from Mississippi. They brought new ways of doing things and new ideas with them, changing the places he knew and loved to better suit the way they wanted to live. And they could do it because they had money. They bought out local politicians and got their way practically every time. And because they had money and spent it freely, they drove up the price of everything, leaving the locals who couldn't afford to keep up out of luck. It got even worse after Katrina hit in 2005.

The devastating hurricane not only leveled a lot of the new development, but finished off for good most of the holdout enclaves of the old Gulf Coast. Federal money and insurance payouts funded a bigger than ever developmental push, and the growth that ensued changed the coast faster in a few years than the entire twenty or so since gambling was legalized. The old marinas and waterfront bars were wiped out, and fancy yacht basins were built in their place. Wayne gave up on keeping a fishing boat in the water ready to go. It simply cost too much for dockage and insurance to be worth it any more. He sold his Pro Line 25 Center Console and went back to mostly fishing the river with his bass boat. But even that kept him too close to the crowds for comfort during his precious time off. Deer hunting was the answer, and to extend the time he could hunt, Wayne took up bowhunting in order to take advantage of the special seasons when firearms weren't allowed. Even that wasn't enough to suit him, so shortly before the blackout changed everything; he'd taken to hunting turkey in the spring and wild hogs in the summer—anything to get him out in the woods as much as possible.

Over the years there had been countless weekend nights spent sitting around a fire at the deer camp with his buddies, usually with the wives and girlfriends left at home. They talked about the problems the country was facing that didn't seem to have a solution, and they worried about the changes they could see coming. It seemed that people who grew up like they did were getting fewer and fewer, especially in other parts of the country where there were not nearly as many places to hunt and fish as in Mississippi. Young people weren't interested in it much anyway, and the gun control and animal rights people were doing their best to steer them away. Wayne and the others could see the writing on the wall; the way of life they loved was threatened more than ever, and they realized they'd better start doing something about it before it was too late. They could see a time coming when it wouldn't even be possible to purchase a shotgun or rifle, so they were determined to get what they needed so they could ensure that their sons would have the chance to hunt and learn to be at home in the outdoors just as they were.

When they started this, they soon realized there was a growing movement among other like-minded people scattered here and there, and it didn't take long to find the information they needed on the Internet and in various books on prepping and long-term survival. Using checklists they found in these resources and coming up with their own from their personal experiences, Wayne and his friends began buying stuff to put into safe storage at the camp. When they first started this, their focus was mainly on guns and ammunition, because that's what they were worried would be in short supply. The more they read and learned, however, the more they realized they needed to add other essential tools as well as food and other supplies to the stockpile as well.

Wayne's experience with firearms was limited to hunting rifles and shotguns, along with a little time spent target shooting with pistols and revolvers. Having worked full time without a break since graduation, he had never served in the military, though he regretted not signing up before marrying the stupid woman that nearly ruined his life. But one of his best friends, Gary Haggard, did serve. As an Army Ranger, Gary saw some serious combat action in Afghanistan, hunting elusive targets that could and did shoot back. Gary's perspective on weapons helped Wayne and his other friends round out their arsenal, and before long, they all felt well-equipped to last a long time even if every gun store in the country was suddenly shut down. Wayne was thankful they had completed this sooner than later, because as it turned out, the option to buy more of *anything* was turned off instantly. It was nothing like the slow loss of rights and changing of laws all of them expected. When the pulse hit, they suddenly found themselves in a world where the land and the things they had built and stored there were the best acquisitions they could have possibly owned, especially compared to almost everyone else.

Wayne had been at the camp when it happened, and didn't even know about it for several days, since the cabin was set up off the grid anyway and he didn't try to keep up with news or anything else from the outside world when he was there. He had his cell phone of course, but when he discovered it was dead, he just cursed the battery that was on its last leg anyway and figured that was the reason. He didn't know about the vehicle situation either, even when he did get ready to leave to go back to Moss Point to get ready for his next hitch. His green-camo '73 Dodge hunting truck started just fine, and it was not until he reached the highway that he figured out something was wrong. By the time he made it to the coast, the situation was really out of control. Tracy was nowhere to be found, and he had not seen her since. He had finally given up on looking for her and figured he would never see her again.

Until today, he hadn't touched a woman since he'd kissed her goodbye that afternoon he'd left for what he thought was a three-day weekend. That had been the first week of spring turkey season, and now, if calendars and laws even mattered any more, it was getting about time for the main fall gun season for deer. Wayne still liked deer hunting as much as ever, but it was about all he did any more, and day after day, life was the same old same old. Finding this girl, April was going to give him a whole new outlook on things. Spending time with her was something to look forward to. It really was the most exciting thing that had happened to Wayne in a long time, and he could barely contain himself as he set out to the south, holding the leash in one hand, giving her a gentle tug to remind her to keep step behind him.

Twelve

EVERY STEP HE TOOK in the direction away from April and Kimberly wrenched at his heart as Mitch ducked and weaved though the undergrowth on his run back to where he'd left Jason waiting. Every second he was not watching he was aware that anything could happen to the two of them in the hands of those men, but he kept telling himself he was doing this the right way. He *needed* that rifle, and Jason needed to know what was going on. Mitch couldn't remember facing a harder decision, but he'd made it and now what he had to do was move as quickly as possible to get Jason and get back to that sandbar so he could pick up the trail before they had time to go far. He didn't see how they could move faster than he could track them, because their speed was going to be limited by April, and she was burdened with the weight and unwieldy way she was carrying Kimberly in her arms. The only thing that would change that was the possibility that the men would get tired of waiting on her and decide to get rid of the child. Mitch hoped they wouldn't do that just yet, but he didn't put anything past them and he knew that the sooner he got back the better. There was no stopping to look and listen any more as he retraced his route downstream along the creek bank. The threat was back there where he'd left it, and Jason was just ahead, hopefully watching and waiting for his return.

Mitch only slowed to a walk once he reached the bay thicket where Jason was hiding. He whispered loudly, calling his name, but to his surprise, got no answer, even on the third attempt. Getting impatient and a little upset that Jason was ignoring him, Mitch called again, still keeping his voice low, but still loud enough for anyone in the thicket to hear. Still nothing! *What in the heck?* Mitch withdrew the arrow he'd placed back in his quiver while running and nocked it to his bowstring. He called again and waited, listening. Jason still did not answer. This was crazy and he didn't have time for it. Mitch made his way to the exact spot where he'd left Jason and saw that he was not there. Why he would have moved when he had explicit instructions to wait in that spot was beyond Mitch's comprehension. Whatever the reason, Mitch was pissed. He examined the leaf litter on the forest floor and saw the disturbed clumps that indicated which way Jason had gone—farther downstream—in the exact opposite direction they needed to be going! Furious, Mitch bent low to study the ground and slowly worked his way along his friend's trail. It was slow going with all the leaves, but he pieced it together and continued until he hit a spot of exposed sand and saw Jason's bootprints, still leading away, farther downstream. Moving as fast as he could but also wary of some new surprise, he ended up covering a couple hundred yards of creek bank before he saw Jason standing next to a big beech tree. His back was to Mitch and he was unaware anyone was behind him. He seemed to be focused on something in the other direction as he stood there, holding the rifle up in a ready position across his chest, slowly stretching and craning his neck as if he were trying to see through the screen of the forest farther downstream.

Mitch stalked closer and cautiously called him by name in a loud whisper, wary of startling him and getting shot as a result. Jason was surprised when he turned around with the rifle at ready, but relaxed when he saw who it was.

"What are you doing?" Mitch demanded, still whispering.

"I heard somebody!" Jason whispered back.

"Not down that way," Mitch said. "They're upstream. I found them. I just came from there!"

"No!" I know there were voices upstream. But I heard voices down this way too! I know I did. They sounded far away, so I just wanted to get a little closer, to see if I could figure it out. But now they've stopped talking."

Mitch looked closely at him and could see that Jason believed what he heard was real. It seemed an unlikely coincidence that there was anyone else out here in the same vicinity at the same time, but Mitch took a couple of minutes to carefully listen for himself after they both stopped talking, just to be sure. When he heard nothing, he grabbed Jason by the sleeve and pulled him close.

"Listen to me, Jason! We've got to go, and now! If there

is somebody down there, it doesn't matter!" Then he quickly filled him in on what was going on back at that sandbar, and how April and Kimberly were in grave danger. Telling Jason to stick close behind him and to be as quiet as possible, Mitch then set out to lead the way back. He kept his bow for now and let Jason carry the rifle until they got there. There was no point in switching, because Jason was not competent with a bow anyway and it would do him little good to carry it.

The extra distance they had to travel now because of Jason's curiosity would give the men more time to get a good head start, but Mitch tried not to think about it as he moved. Jason had failed him in a way, by not staying put as he'd been instructed, but Mitch knew he was just trying to help. Even though he was positive what he'd heard was real, Mitch doubted it was really voices. The excitement of the morning's tracking and the real voices they both *had* heard had obviously made an impression on his friend. Sitting there alone in the clump of bay trees, his mind had surely been playing tricks on him as he waited and listened, soaking in all the sounds of the forest that surrounded him. Mitch knew how the trickle and splash of moving water could create the illusion of voices. A fallen branch could get caught in an eddy or area of fast water, where it would be repeatedly dunked and lifted, making all sorts of gurgling and voice-like sounds that could be quite convincing. Mitch had heard it himself all too often, and he knew too that such sounds gave rise to most of superstitions of spirits and other unseen creatures that were a part of forest legends and myths everywhere.

Mitch no longer had any fear of the unknown in the wild, whether in daylight or the middle of a dark, moonless night. He knew that few people in modern America, or what had been modern America before the great blackout, were as comfortable and at ease alone in the woods as he. He could give his dad much of the credit for that, but even Doug Henley, as knowledgeable a woodsman as a man could be, still preferred coming home to a real house and sleeping indoors with his family. Mitch, however, shunned the artificial, manmade world, as often as possible even before and now he knew that with each passing month it would be harder than ever to go back to that kind of life when and if technology were restored. If not for his little sister and her friends, Mitch figured he would probably be ranging far and wide up and down Black Creek, living the life of a nomadic hunter and calling no particular place home. It was a long-held fantasy for him before—to experience a life like that—but even with the farm to go back to at night, his new reality was close enough to that dream that he didn't feel he was missing much.

But none of that was on his mind now. What Mitch thought about as he led the way with Jason on his heels was how he was going to deal with these four men. He had no illusion that he could somehow rescue April without extreme and unhesitating violence, and that likely meant killing all four, preferably before they realized what was happening. It would be easier if it were April alone, but with Kimberly at risk too and April's natural instincts as a mother to put her child's life first, it was going to take carefully considered action to pull off a rescue. He simply couldn't afford to screw this up. Saving April only to have something happen to her child would be worse than doing nothing at all. Mitch knew it would destroy her, and he didn't even want to go there in his mind.

The route Mitch took to get back to where he had watched what was taking place on the sandbar was as direct as possible. This meant he did not follow all the looping bends of Black Creek, because that would have taken much longer. Mitch didn't give this a second thought until they closed in on the sandbar. Stopping to look and listen, motioning Jason to silence behind him, he determined that the men, along with April and Kimberly were indeed gone before he approached closer. Moving faster now, they pushed the rest of the way through until they came in view of the sandbar, and Mitch saw that David was still lying where he had been before, unmoving in the sand beside the smoldering campfire. But that was something he expected and was not the main thing that caught his attention. What really surprised him was that the aluminum canoe was gone! How that could be, he had no idea. He had seen them preparing to set out on foot, April tied by the neck with a rope held by the leader. And Mitch had waited long enough to watch them disappear into the forest. So who had taken the canoe? He couldn't imagine that it had been anyone else, and he had seen before that it was high enough up on the sandbar and even secured to a bush, so he knew it could not have drifted away on its own.

The men couldn't have changed their minds and decided to float downriver either, because there was no way they could all fit in it even without April and Kimberly. Mitch cursed his failure to stick to the creek bank on the way back to this place. If he had, he would have seen the canoe go by and would know the answer to this puzzle. He hadn't expected this. It was another variable and he began to wonder if he'd made a huge mistake to ever let April and Kimberly out of his sight to begin with.

But mistake or not, what was done, was done, and there was no time to waste on regret. Leading Jason to a place he knew just downstream, where the creek was shallow enough to wade, Mitch made his way across to the opposite bank as fast as he could. He had to get to work deciphering all those tracks in the sand so he could figure out exactly what was going on. With no time to waste, he asked Jason to check and see if David was alive or dead, while he bent to the task before him.

Thirteen

APRIL SAT AS STILL as she possibly could in the bow of the canoe, terrified that she might do something to cause it to tip over, drowning Kimberly as well as herself. Her ankles were lashed together and this lashing was in turn secured to the seat thwart beneath her. Kimberly was cradled in her arms, but her wrists were bound and the only thing keeping her baby from falling out was the way she was balanced there on her forearms.

She couldn't turn around to look back over her shoulder without leaning the boat. Wayne, the apparent ringleader of the four men her family had the misfortune to cross paths with in this lonely place, had made sure she would not attempt to escape. He had secured her and placed Kimberly there before they shoved off, warning her that any sudden move on her part would result in a capsize, which she and her child might not survive. April knew he wasn't kidding. Even if he tried to cut her loose in the event of an accidental spill, it might be impossible to do so fast enough, especially for Kimberly, who would be swept away in the current. He had April just where he wanted her, and all she could do was sit there and wonder how far he was taking her and what would happen when they got there.

At first, she'd thought they were all going to be traveling on foot to wherever that was, and that's the way they started out. But they had not gone a quarter of mile before April slipped while climbing a slick clay bank when they had to cross a deep gully. When she felt her foot go out from under her, she had grabbed the rope around her neck in one hand to keep from getting strangled, while clinging tightly to Kimberly with the other. As a result, she could do little to break her fall when Wayne dropped the rope from where he was standing, already atop the bank. April tried to roll with it and she did manage to keep from dropping Kimberly or landing on top of her, but her right foot got turned under her as she tumbled. A sharp pain shooting through her ankle told her she'd twisted it hard, and sure enough, when she tried to stand back up at the bottom of the ditch, it hurt too much to put her weight on it.

Wayne scrambled back down the slope and grabbed the loose end of the rope. "What'd you do that for? Are you okay?"

"I don't think I can climb out of here. I turned my ankle."

"Dammit, what did I tell you, Wayne?" the one he'd called Gary demanded from the other side, where he and the rest of the party were waiting to cross. "We can't take her all the way back. I knew something like this would happen. We shouldn't have even tried."

"She *is* going with us! Or with me anyway. If the rest of you don't want to help, I'll get her there by myself!"

"How?" One of the other men asked. "She can't even walk now." He looked to be the youngest of the group; April guessed only a few years older than her. He had been staring at her with no attempt to conceal his lust since the four of them had first appeared. April knew exactly what would happen if it was up to him, or any of them other than Wayne, for that matter.

But Wayne ignored him and turned to April. "Give me the little girl. I won't hurt her. I'll help you back up to the top and we'll have a look at that ankle."

"Just leave us here," April pleaded. "We're only gonna slow you down. I can't walk. We'll stay here by the river until my ankle is better."

"Staying here is not an option. I'm not leaving either of you."

"If she can't walk, and walk fast enough to keep up, then we've got to leave her," Gary said. He turned to April: "You'd better figure out fast how to walk with that turned ankle, or you're going to die here; you and your little girl."

"We're not leaving her here, Gary. So shut up with the threats and give me a hand. Help me get her back up there."

April refused to hand Kimberly over to Wayne, but she did allow him to help her up the steep bank, knowing she couldn't do it by herself. Reluctantly, she put one arm over his shoulder for support, while Gary grabbed her from the other side and they pulled and steadied her until she was on top. She then leaned against a tree and slowly eased herself to a sitting position, keeping a firm hold on Kimberly the entire time.

The swelling that had already started around her bare ankle was obvious to all of them, so they knew she wasn't faking it. She was in real pain too, and she wondered what this was going to mean for her and her child. There was no way she could hike cross-country like this, even if she didn't have to carry Kimberly. Wayne was clearly determined not to leave her, but if the other three had their way, they would do what they wanted to her now and be done with her.

"Look at that ankle, Wayne! You say we're not going to leave her here, so what are you gonna do, carry her?" This was the youngest one again, the one who hadn't stopped looking at her since he'd first seen her.

"She can't walk. I got that. But that doesn't mean there's not a way. That's your problem, Jared. You just don't stop to think about all the options. Now, which way are we going anyway?"

April watched as Jared tried to figure out what Wayne was getting at.

"Let me help you, Jared. We're going *downstream*. Now what does that mean? It means that if she can't walk, she can *float*."

"We can't all fit in that one damned canoe, if that's what you're suggesting!"

"No, but it'll carry her and the kid, along with me in it to paddle."

"Splitting up would be stupid!" Gary said. "Why would you want to take a risk like that over a female? I know it's been a long time, but damn, you'll be a sitting duck out there, paddling that canoe down the middle of the creek!"

"Sitting duck for who? Have you seen anybody else other than these three since we came upriver?"

"No, but that doesn't mean somebody hasn't seen us. And even if they haven't you could come around a bend any time and run into somebody either on the bank or in another canoe or boat. Having a girl like that with you is just going to make you a target, just like that son-of-a-bitch we left laying back there on the sandbar was for us."

"Look, I don't like the idea of splitting up either, Gary. But this time it makes sense. You know damned well she can't walk with that ankle, and even if she hadn't fallen, she would still slow us down too much, carrying that kid through these woods. We've got a lot of miles to cover, you know that."

"I would have left the kid back there with her daddy if it was up to me."

April shuddered when she heard Gary suggest that again, because she knew full well that he meant it. She knew that none of the others wanted to bring Kimberly along, but Wayne seemed to think he could get her to comply with his wishes if they did. He was right, too. April would do anything to protect her child, and if they even tried to leave her behind or hurt her, she was determined they would have to kill her right then and there because she wasn't going anywhere without her Kimberly.

But once again, whether the others liked it or not, it appeared Wayne was going to get his way. For whatever reason, he was the one calling the shots, even though he looked to be about the same age as Gary and Gary seemed to challenge him at every turn. She figured the two of them were around thirty, give or take a year or two. From their ongoing discussion she gathered there were others in their band of outlaws or whatever it was they were, waiting somewhere else for them to return. The idea of having to try and escape from a larger group than these four certainly made her uneasy, but at this point April couldn't think of a thing she could do other than go along willingly. As long as she and Kimberly were together, she knew they at least had a chance. That was far better than what had happened to David. Though she was not in love with him any more, if she'd even ever been, he was still Kimberly's father and he was still a friend and companion, whether they argued all the time or not. She was saddened to have to accept the truth that he was dead or would soon be dead, and that there was nothing she could do for him.

When it became apparent that Wayne was going to get his way in regard to splitting up from the others, April wondered what would have happened to her and Kimberly if the canoe had not been an option. Her ankle was hurting so bad she could barely put her weight on it, much less walk. It would be impossible for her to travel on foot, even if it were a matter of life or death, and even if she did not have to carry Kimberly. And even if she were not injured, walking any distance through these woods carrying a child would be exhausting.

On the other hand, sitting in the canoe took no effort, but it was much more dangerous for both of them considering the way she was lashed to the boat. She just hoped Wayne had enough experience in canoes to not do something stupid. The creek was full of hidden stumps and snags, many of them in areas of swift water where it took skill with a paddle to avoid them. She and David had come close to capsizing several times among just such obstacles during their journey downstream from Brooklyn.

When they shoved off into the current and Wayne began paddling, the final agreement with the other three was that they would stick as close to the left bank as possible, with a rendezvous to camp together each evening at pre-arranged locations.

April gathered this was both to provide backup for Wayne in the event they encountered other river travelers, and perhaps, because Gary and the others didn't want to let him out of their sight for too long for fear they would miss out. She certainly wasn't looking forward to nightfall and the prospect of camping with any of them, whether the whole group or just Wayne alone. It was a heck of a predicament she was in, but April had been in many bad predicaments in the past seven months. As she sat there and watched the dense walls of forest slide by on both sides as the canoe cut through the water, she reminded herself that she and Kimberly were both still alive and still together. And while they were, there was always hope.

Fourteen

WHEN MITCH REACHED THE sandbar he found such a mess of confusing footprints the story they told was practically impossible to decipher. The problem was that April and David had been walking all over it since at least the afternoon before, and then the four strangers had trampled it after that. There were so many tracks on top of tracks that they all blended together, especially in the dry, sugary-white quartz sand that was so deep the prints began to fill almost as soon as they were made. The first place Mitch looked was in the area where the canoe had been resting. There were drag marks where it had been pulled up there and more where it had been launched, but the footprints all around them were overlapping and confusing. There were certainly some that were a size that had to be April's, but so many boot prints over them that he could not find clear evidence to show if she had been near the boat again or not since they arrived. Instead of wasting more time trying to decide, Mitch thought his efforts would be better spent starting someplace he *knew* she had been—at the edge of the woods where he had last seen her before she disappeared into the foliage.

"Hey, this guy's still alive, Mitch! He's breathing and I can feel a pulse!"

Jason's announcement had a tone of urgency, but at least he'd done as Mitch had warned and kept his voice to barely over a whisper. There was no way of knowing how far the party may have gone and they couldn't risk being heard at this point. Anything Mitch was going to do for April and Kimberly was going to depend on the element of surprise considering how the numbers were so heavily in favor of her captors.

Mitch was glad to hear this news, though. He took a minute to go see for himself, kneeling in the sand and turning the unconscious man's head just enough to see the knot on the side that had been struck. From the way it had sounded on impact, he was truly surprised that David's scull was not literally caved-in. But Jason was right; he was alive and truly lucky to be so.

"Do you think he'll wake up?" Jason asked.

"I don't know. Probably, but it might take a while. He's bound to have a severe concussion. He could stay in a coma or go back into one, even if he does come to. But it's not as bad as I expected. He may be just fine."

"What are we gonna do with him?"

"We'll get him to the other side of the creek, at least. I'll help you before I go, and you can go back to the house for the others. But first, I've got to try and figure out what happened here. Try splashing some water on his face while you wait and see if that helps. I've got to get back on this trail."

Mitch forced back the growing anxiety he felt as he crouched low, making his way to the edge of the woods while visually scanning every print he could see in the sand. He could clearly see the place where April had stood while the one man tied the rope around her neck, and leading away from there, the mostly single-file tracks the five of them made crossing a muddy area of low ground between the sandbar and the higher ground of the top bank beyond. The tracks in the mud were smeared and those of the men in the rear covered most of April's but it was clear she had walked this way with them. There were no prints going back in the opposite direction, either. It was a confusing situation, but Mitch knew he didn't have time to be confused. Every minute that went by while he was trying to figure this out was a minute that April was being carried farther and farther away from him—and a minute that anything could be happening to her and Kimberly.

Mitch made up his mind then and there. He would follow this trail wherever it led. There was no way the men who made it could get away from him, but a canoe, on the other hand, left no tracks. He knew it was possible that April was in it, but if she was, there was no way for it to go but downstream or upstream, and the latter was unlikely, considering the current. If she were on foot as she had been when he'd last seen her, however, the trail could lead most anywhere. He had to follow up on that probability first, and he knew he had no time to waste. He made his way back to where Jason was still trying to revive David and saw that he had not been successful.

"Let's get him across the creek, Jason. I've got to get moving, and now!"

Mitch slung his bow across his back and grabbed David from under his arms, instructing Jason to get his feet. His limp body was heavy, but they managed to get him to the shallow area they had crossed earlier, and with a combination of floating and carrying, pulled him across to the bank that was on the same side as the Henley farm.

"I don't know how long I'll be gone, Jason. I'm going to be depending on you to look after Lisa and the others, and I know you can do it. When you get them and come back here for David, make sure you get him back to the house as fast as possible. You can rig up a travois like we've used to haul deer. You know how to do it. The main thing is just don't leave the house unattended for too long. And don't leave him out here after dark if you can help it. It won't take long for the dogs to find him out here."

Mitch didn't want to leave Jason unarmed when he took the AR-15, so he unbuckled his belt and removed the holstered .357 Magnum revolver he'd been wearing as a back up.

"Keep this handy. You probably won't need it, but it's better to have it than not. How many mags did you bring for the AR?"

Jason dug into the deep pockets of his cargo pants and pulled out two. They were each standard thirty-rounders. Another one was already locked into the magazine well of the rifle. Mitch checked to make sure Jason had already chambered the first round from that one. He figured ninety rounds was far more than he would need, but he would certainly take them all and if Jason had brought more, that would have been even better. He slung the carbine across his back and removed the bow to carry in hand. The AR could be brought into play quickly from almost any carry position, but if he needed to utilize the silence of the bow in a hurry, it was best to carry it at the ready, an arrow nocked on the string just as he always did while hunting. And this was indeed a hunt, but a hunt in which a lot more hung in the balance than if the prey was merely food. Today Mitch was hunting men; men that would kill him if they saw him and men that would do as they pleased with April and Kimberly if he did not kill them first. He intended to do nothing less and the sooner he could make it happen the better.

"Good luck," Jason whispered. "I wish I was going with you. The odds would be better than four to one, at least."

"Numbers aren't everything, Jason. I don't intend to give them a chance to use that to their advantage. With any luck at all, they'll never know what hit them."

"Still, I wish I could be there."

"Just try to get back to the house as fast as you can. Lisa

and Stacy will be wondering what's going on. I don't want them to get any ideas about trying to come out here and find out. And David needs to be moved there. April's going to be relieved to find out he's alive when I bring her and her child back. He is the little girl's father, after all."

Mitch remembered the day he'd met David and Kimberly for the first time. After all those days traveling alone with April, though so much danger and adventure, finally arriving at that church and realizing their journey was over had been painful. Seeing her child in real life and meeting the man who'd fathered her, the reality sunk in for Mitch that his journey with April was really over. He knew he would miss her when they parted, and he did. He'd thought about her constantly the first few days, and only a little less over the subsequent weeks. Finally, the day-to-day challenges of survival and looking out for his sister and the others had pushed her memory farther back in his mind, but there were still times he wondered how she and her family were doing. Seeing her again, especially out here was a total shock, and something he'd never expected. Obviously, David was still very much a part of her life or he wouldn't be here, so for her sake, Mitch was glad he was alive. After all she'd been through and was going through now, she didn't need any more tragedy in her life. He was determined to bring her and Kimberly back to the farm, and finding David there would only add to her relief.

Mitch bent over him once more to check his vital signs.

110

His pulse was still strong and he was breathing as before. Chances were, he would come to sooner or later.

"I'm on my way, Jason. Now get moving and get to the house and tell Lisa and the others I will be back as soon as possible, but don't worry if it's longer than you think it should be. I won't be returning without April and that little girl!"

With that, Mitch gave Jason a final handshake and then turned to wade back across Black Creek. He didn't pause to wave or even look back when he reached the other side. He entered the woods and made his way directly to the last place he'd stopped when examining the tracks, and then set out in pursuit.

When the trail led to the higher and drier ground on the true top bank, well above the stream's high water line, actual footprints became almost non-existent. It was to be expected, but again, looking for the path of least resistance kept him on track. By simply going the way he knew most people would pick, he could occasionally see where feet had shuffled through the leaf litter and small forest floor plants were crushed or bent. Just as they were before they came here and took April captive, the four men were traveling without concern of being followed. Mitch knew they probably thought they were so deep in the woods that they had nothing to worry about. Little did they know that they were being hunted by a predator they could not escape, and that their vicious actions had guaranteed they would receive no

INTO THE RIVER LANDS

mercy when he found them.

Fifteen

GARY HAGGARD LED THE way downstream, doing his best to stick reasonably close to the creek, but frequently having to take a wide detour around thickets and areas of dense briars and other undergrowth. These forestlands along this stretch of Black Creek were not like this before Hurricane Katrina devastated them when it swept through Mississippi in 2005. Gary knew this, because it had been one of his favorite places to deer hunt before he went to Afghanistan in 2003. Back then, most of the stream bank here was shaded in mature forests of tall pines and mixed hardwoods, the canopy shutting out most of the light and allowing little undergrowth. It had been a beautiful place; one of the few areas of such extensive old-growth forest left in the state, and walking and hunting in it had been a pleasure.

But one-hundred-mile-an-hour plus winds had wreaked havoc on a lot of it, blowing down many of the tallest trees and breaking the tops off many more. The holes and gaps created by this destruction opened up the ground to sunlight in the same way logging operations did in the cutover woods found practically everywhere else in the state. Rampant vegetation grew where once there had only been shade with moss and ferns. Blackberry briars, privet hedge and bushes and small seedlings of every species shot up in the openings and grew into tangles and thickets, each species trying to choke out the others. It made walking in a straight line just about impossible, and traveling through such damaged forestland on foot was a march through hell. The only thing that helped was a sharp machete to cut a path through the worst of it.

Gary was used to it, of course. Just like Wayne and the others, he literally lived in the woods these days and spent most of his time hunting or bushwhacking when they weren't in the cabin at the camp. But this had been the longest expedition they'd undertaken since moving permanently to the hunting club land after the blackout, and he was ready to get back to familiar turf and take a break. This trip was essentially the same as the long-range recon missions he'd done so many of over there, just different terrain and a different purpose. And though in those missions he knew going in that he was going to get shot at if seen, it was about the same here. The only difference was they had *not* been seen so far.

There had been more than a few run-ins on the hunting camp property though. The problem there was that even though it was in the middle of a huge expanse of woods, it was still too damned close to the coast. That's why they were here in the first place—scouting upriver—looking to the future to try and figure out what they were going to do in the longer term. When everything hit the fan in the beginning, it didn't seem likely the situation would last as long as it did or get as bad as it had. Now, it didn't seem likely things would ever go back to the way they were before. It wouldn't be smart to just sit back and not consider all the options and conduct some advance planning.

It was too bad these woods were no longer the forest paradise Gary remembered. It would have been the perfect place to relocate. He knew they still might have to do it anyway. Travel by canoe or small boat was still easy enough, even if walking was not. And the game was still plentiful here; this trip had confirmed that. They had seen little sign of other human presence, other than the chance discovery of that unlucky family camped on the sandbar. Gary couldn't believe someone as pathetic as that guy had survived long enough to get this far. Only in the world back then, before the big change could guys like him live long enough to mate, especially with a girl like that one.

Gary still smiled to himself when he replayed in his mind the image of her busting Wayne's nose and putting him on his ass in the sand. She was one tough little chick! She had put his buddy in quite a spot, and Gary knew how he felt. He knew Wayne was trying to prove something now, but he figured it wouldn't last. He just wanted to tame that little tigress on his own terms to save face, but it wasn't really like him to be selfish. They had been through a lot together and

Gary already owed him favors. As far as he was concerned, no woman was worth fighting a good friend over. But taking out her sorry excuse for a husband? Gary had no qualms about that. The way he saw it, he was doing her favor. Gary had little sympathy for anyone outside their small band of survivors these days. He'd seen plenty of innocent people die horrible deaths long before this event put his own country into a state of anarchy. A soldier learned to harden himself to such things early on if he wanted to do his job. The lives that really mattered were those of the other men in his unit. Now, for all practical purposes, *everyone* else was the enemy.

He wasn't crazy about the idea of splitting up the group and Wayne being out there alone with the woman and kid in the canoe. He thought Wayne was being a little stupid for taking such a risk to get her back to the camp, but it wasn't worth a huge argument either. Maybe he was right. Maybe a woman like her would be an asset later on if they kept her alive. She would have to adapt if she wanted to live, especially if she wanted them to let her keep the kid. Gary figured it didn't much matter to him one way or another, as long as he didn't have to feed her. Wayne would either find the burden worth it or he wouldn't, and he would do something about it then.

Jared and Paul were sure unhappy about Wayne keeping her to himself, but Gary had finally had enough and told them to shut up and forget it. They all had a long trek ahead of them, and he was tired of hearing it. Besides, just because they hadn't seen anybody else in these woods, that didn't mean there were no dangers. It was best to travel in silence, just as if they were expecting an ambush at any moment.

Gary kept his custom Bulgarian AK at the ready in it's two-point tactical sling in front of his chest, and he kept his cutting with the machete to the bare minimum, picking a way around, instead of through, the worst of the thickets. When he did have to use the blade, to clear a briar vine or branch, he sliced through it at an angle with an upward stroke. Kept shaving sharp at all times, the 22-inch Collins would part most of them in a single pass this way. Gary had long ago learned that such an upward slash cut the cleanest and with the least blade ring or whack upon impact.

Machete or not, it was completely impractical to follow the creek bend-for-bend, so even though they were walking at roughly the same speed as Wayne would be paddling, they could not keep up with him or stay anywhere near visual or audible contact range. That just simply didn't work in this kind of woodland. The best they could do was agree to rendezvous at recognizable landmarks, which were few and far between on a creek that looked mostly the same for mile after winding mile.

The first such spot where they planned to meet for the night was at a sandbar on the same side they were walking, just downstream from the next bridge crossing. This crossing was a county road that likely had little traffic even before the blackout, and there had been nothing in the area before other than a remote Forest Service campground on the creek bank nearby. Finding it would be easy whether they were near the creek or not, because they would have to cross the road at some point and paralleling it from the other side back to the creek would take them right there. Once they met up with Wayne again and made sure everything was going okay with him in the canoe, they could decide on the next rendezvous, probably at the state highway bridge that was another ten miles downstream beyond that one.

It would be a bit of a pain to arrange all these checkpoints, but by doing so, they would all arrive back at the land at roughly the same time. And if Wayne did run into trouble out there on the creek, chances were they'd be close enough by to help him out of a bind before it was too late. Gary knew there was no other option than the canoe if they were going to take the girl and her kid that far. Even if she hadn't screwed up her ankle, she might not be able to make it carrying such a burden. They were looking at a solid three-day trek, maybe four if there were any more delays. It was a good thing for her that the canoe was available, and that Wayne had plans for her that extended beyond what he could have done right then and there.

And so it was that Gary Haggard focused all his attention on the way forward, despite all his training and experience that should have kept his mind and senses open to other considerations. His thoughts were completely occupied with keeping his eyes and ears open for danger lurking in the woods ahead, as well as working out the route through all of these obstacles. His immediate goal was reaching that first check-in point before dark, and knowing Jared and Paul were close behind him, where they were supposed to be, he had little reason to concern himself with his back trail. He knew they would eventually return to this more remote area of the creek, maybe even permanently, but for now he was looking forward to getting back to the relative comfort of the cabin and their familiar land. Just like during the war over there, it was always a relief when a patrol was over, and this one seemed over already now that they were on the return leg to home turf. He had little reason to expect anything else would happen that would be half as exciting as this morning's encounter on the sandbar.

Sixteen

WAYNE PARKER STEERED THE canoe for the bank and ran the bow up on a narrow strip of sand in the shade of a big cypress tree. He couldn't stand it another minute. The little girl had started up crying again and nothing would stop her. April kept trying to sooth her with reassuring words, all the while begging him to pull over and let her give her child something to eat. Wayne didn't see any way around it. They were making way too much noise and his threats to get them to shut up weren't doing a damned bit of good.

"She's hungry and she's scared to death! Any child would be scared in this situation, even you should know that! She's never going to stop crying unless I can hold her in my arms and touch her. I can't do that with my hands tied. She can do this for hours. Days even! Believe me, I'm her mother. I should know!"

"Fine then! But if you don't get her quiet, we'll be leaving her behind. So whatever you're going to do, you'd better make it work, and fast!"

Wayne stepped out of the canoe and opened the Spyderco folder April had pulled on him in their scuffle. The blade was honed to a razor's edge and it went through the multiple wraps of three-eight's inch nylon rope around April's wrists like they weren't even there. It didn't bother Wayne to cut them, because it was just cheap line anyway, part of the bow painter supplied with the rental canoe, many more feet of which was coiled and lying on the bottom of the boat. He didn't want to be fumbling with untying knots, especially now that he was handling his captive alone. He'd already seen what she was capable of, and figured having the knife open and ready and in his hand would give her pause. It wasn't worth taking any chances and he didn't really want to have to seriously hurt either her or the kid. Before he freed her he made that point clear too, warning her that Kimberly would be the one to pay if she tried anything stupid. He didn't think she would take that risk, and he was right. He opened one of the MREs from his pack and gave it to April. The little girl was obviously hungry from the way she gobbled up the portion of peanut butter inside.

When they shoved off again, April was sitting in the bottom of the boat, facing him, her back against the thwart of the bow seat, the rope about her neck tied to it with just enough slack to allow her to sit upright and breathe easy. Although her hands were free, he felt she was still pretty secure. Being tied to the boat by the neck was a good deterrent to prevent her from doing something stupid, like causing him to dump it while they were moving. She wouldn't have a chance to save herself and Kimberly at the same time,

SCOTT B. WILLIAMS

and she had to realize that. Untied or not, her hands were occupied anyway, because in this position she could hold Kimberly close, and finally, the squalling kid had settled down and shut her mouth.

Wayne knew that the child was all that mattered to this woman. He knew she hated the fact that she was stuck in that position facing him, and that he was staring at her all the while as he steered and paddled, but as long as she had that little girl in her arms, she would endure anything. She was good mother, as well as a fighter and a survivor. She had exactly the traits Wayne felt a woman should have to live in this harsh new reality. The more he looked at her, the more he came to realize that she was just about perfect for him. Now that the screaming kid was quiet, he could finally talk to her. The way he figured it, three or four days of floating down the river would give him a good start on getting to know her.

"So April, how old is Kimberly, exactly?"

She said nothing, nor did she look up at him. She had not looked up at him once since they had started back downriver with her in this new seating arrangement.

"I know you don't want to talk to me, but you will. I want to know everything about you. I want to hear your story, where you're from, where you were when the solar flares hit…. I want to know what you did that day and how you survived this long since. And what I really want to know is why you ended up out here in this canoe. Where were you

123

two going and what did you expect to find out here? How did you expect to take care of your baby way out here in these woods alone, and with a husband who couldn't even hunt, let alone defend you?"

April still ignored him.

"Did you not know Black Creek runs for more than a hundred miles through pretty much nothing but national forest land and other remote country? Or did you even know the name of the creek you were on? Were you hoping going downriver would take you someplace better? You had to know that reaching the coast wouldn't do you much good. That's where I'm from, and let me tell you; it's the last place you want to be right now."

"We weren't going to the coast," April said, finally breaking the silence but not looking up at him as she spoke. "We were looking for my friend, and believe me, we would be safe with him if we had found him."

"Out here? On the creek? Just where does this friend of yours live? We haven't seen much sign of life out here in more than a week."

"He's here, and not far either. You're lucky you *didn't* see him, because he wouldn't like the fact that you're here, trespassing and hunting on his family land."

"His family land? This is national forest land. Public land, as if it even mattered now anyway."

"Not all of it. You just think it is because you've been following the creek. No one could find his land though if they didn't know where to look, but he keeps an eye on who's coming and going along this creek."

"Well, I don't see him now, do you? Where was he this morning when we found you on that sandbar? I think your imaginary friend may have overslept just like your husband, do you suppose?"

"Screw you! I don't even want to be reminded about what you did to David! If it wasn't for my child, you would have had to leave me there dead too before I would have gotten in this boat with you!"

"But you *do* have your child, April. And if you want to keep it that way, you'll just sit there and not rock the boat."

Wayne knew she would comply. It seemed to him that she was not as upset about the way they had left her husband as she should be. He wondered if the man lying back there in the sand really was her husband or if she had just made that up. It didn't really matter to him one way or the other. He knew it could be too, just that she had simply seen so much death and suffering since the lights went out that she was numb to it by now. If that was it, she was not alone, that was for sure.

Wayne had long reached that point, in fact, he'd reached it by the end of the first week when he'd finally made his way back down to the coast only to find Tracy missing. Not knowing where she had gone or what had happened to her was one thing, but then he had gone to his boyhood home in Moss Point and found his parents dead, murdered in their living room, apparently from repeated blows with a blunt object. All because somebody thought they needed the perfectly running 1968 Ford pickup parked in the carport more than his 74-year-old father did. Wayne spent most of a day digging their graves with a shovel in the backyard, and then he had set out to return to the woods. There were run-ins with desperate types who were far less prepared than he and his friends at the hunting camp, and Wayne showed no mercy as he dealt with them as ruthlessly as they no doubt had done with their victims. Killing people came easy to him now, easier than killing game really. The deer and other animals he took for food were just unlucky to be in the wrong place at the wrong time, and taking their lives was just a simple necessity of survival. Killing looters and gang members was different. It seemed most people he met these days *needed* killing for one reason or another. The man with April, whether he was really her husband or not, had not really done anything wrong, at least that Wayne knew of. But he was stupid; stupid and incompetent and simply a victim of natural selection in a world where the stupid and the weak were getting scarcer by the day.

He could have left April and her kid there too, and maybe that's what the other guys wanted, but his hatred of humanity did not extend to everyone. A woman like her would be a good thing to have around. He firmly believed that in these circumstances, no matter what he had to do to make her comply and go with him back to the camp, she would come around eventually. She would warm up to him and the others as well and be grateful just to have a safe place to live with plenty of food for her and her child. Wayne was certain of this, because what other choice did she really have? He'd seen enough by now to know that no matter what people said, or what they believed, when conditions were hard enough, they would break down and submit. And this April, no matter how strong-willed she was, would be no exception.

Seventeen

WHEN HE LEFT THE sandbar and entered the heavy woods in the direction he had seen the men go with April and Kimberly, Mitch found plenty of evidence of their passage to know for sure he was on the trail. The most obvious signs were fresh-cut briar vines and small branches still oozing fresh sap where they had been sliced through with a sharp blade. And there were more subtle signs that did not escape his practiced eye; things like clumps of overturned pine needles and leaf litter kicked up by a shuffling boot. It was easy to see they were fresh by the still damp undersides that had been holding moisture against the earth before being disturbed. Actual footprints mattered little to Mitch; he knew he would find them again from time to time, as there would be many areas of mud and sand that the group would have to cross.

He came to the first such place not far at all from the sandbar where the trail began. It was a deep gully that would be half full of water during rainy times such as late winter and early spring, but now it was mostly dry in the bottom, with only a few puddles of still water remaining in the deeper holes. The banks were steep and slick with mud and clay. Deep ditches and gullies like this one were typical of the many obstacles that anyone attempting to follow the creek on foot would encounter.

Mitch knelt at the edge and examined the tracks, seeing a long slide mark from near the top on his side that went all the way to the bottom of the ditch. That one of them had slipped while climbing down was not surprising. Mitch had done the same many times while scrambling in and out of such gullies. Some of them in the area were deep and with near vertical banks, making them impossible to climb into or out of without using exposed roots and the trunks of small saplings for handholds. There was nothing to hold onto at this particular spot April's captors had picked for crossing however, and he figured they probably didn't want to spend the time to look for a better route.

Mitch carefully climbed down to the bottom to see if he could determine which one of them it was that slipped, thinking that because of the way April was carrying Kimberly, it could have been her. When he got to the dry streambed, the footprints he found were a confusing mess that was impossible to decipher. He could clearly see one set of tracks continuing across and up the opposite bank, which was equally steep. Whoever made them had difficulty going up that way because each print was smeared with slip marks on the downhill side, leaving little indication as to the type or size shoe or boot that made them. Mitch figured it was probably one of the men, because in the bottom of the gully he saw that there were many more tracks leading downstream, in the direction of Black Creek. Whoever had climbed up straight across obviously had a difficult time of it, and the others went looking for a better place to gain the top bank on the other side.

Mitch bent low and followed the main group until he came to sandy wash some three feet wide in the bottom of the ditch. Here the individual footprints were distinct, and it was here that he finally found what he was looking for. Dropping to his hands and knees in the wet sand, he examined a print that was clearly made by a foot that was significantly smaller than any of the others. Tracing the distinct outline made by the edges of her shoe sent shivers down Mitch's spine. April had been right here, her foot landing in this exact spot he was touching now! This knowledge was one of the things he loved about tracking, whether following the trail of an animal or a fellow human being. The tracks told a story he could read like a book, and there was no question that the one he sought had occupied this exact same space where he now knelt, and just a short time prior. If only she could know he was here; that he was right on her trail not far behind and coming to get her! Surely that knowledge would give her hope in a situation where she must have little left. Mitch couldn't imagine what must be going through April's mind right now, alone with her child in the hands of four armed men she had little chance of escaping on her own. She would be frightened for herself but even more so for Kimberly, and she would surely be grieving for what happened to her little girl's father. Mitch knew she would be wondering where they were being taken and what their fate would be when they got there. She would be sick with worry for her child, but he was determined to catch up quickly and make sure her time of distress was as short as possible.

Looking for her next track beyond the left shoe print he was touching, Mitch could not find the expected one from the right shoe in the place it should have been. The tracks of the men were all over the place as well, and maybe one had landed over April's, but as he looked farther down the streambed, he kept finding her left prints, but never any from her right. As he considered this, he dropped to his knees again to look closer. The left prints he found were deep, and always beside them where the boot prints of one of the men, both the left and the right. Mitch began to think that his first assumption that it could have been April who slipped and fell down the bank was correct. If so, had she injured her right foot or leg so that she was unable to walk on it? Would that explain why she and the others had not attempted to climb the opposite bank?

Mitch followed the trail until the ditch ended where it opened up and entered Black Creek. There was a small sandbar at the mouth and the prints here told the same story. There were several more made by April's left shoe, but not a single one from the right. The tracks led right to the water's edge and there, cut deeply into the edge of the sandbar, was the telltale V-shaped groove where the bow of a canoe had recently landed. Mitch's heart sank with the realization of what had happened. This explained why the canoe was missing from the sandbar where April and David left it. She must have fallen hard enough that she was unable to walk without help. That was why he had not seen any prints from her right shoe. One of the men had to have been helping her along until they reached the water's edge. Another of them must have gone upstream to get the canoe, paddling it back and then landing here to pick her up. Mitch checked the sand and mud along the bank to confirm this, and sure enough, he found the boot prints from one man heading back upstream.

He could find no evidence that April had gone anywhere other than straight into the creek. They must have put her and Kimberly into the canoe and one of them had set off with the two of them, paddling it downriver. There was really no other explanation. Mitch checked every track on the sandbar and followed those that doubled back until he found the place where the others had continued on foot. It took him a few minutes to find a good spot where the tracks were clear, but finally he came to another mud flat where he could identify three distinct sets of footprints, all made by man-sized boots. At this point, there was no doubt in his mind. These three had continued downstream on foot, following the creek along their original route before the mishap at the gully. But April and Kimberly were in the canoe with the forth. It was not what he'd expected when he first picked up the trail where it began at the sandbar. Mitch had been confident that four men and a woman would leave a trail he could not lose, but he had not foreseen the possibility of the group splitting up. People on foot could be tracked but canoes could not. And April was in the canoe rather than with the group still traveling on foot.

His mind was racing with the implications of this and Mitch felt the pressure to make a quick decision. Surely since the four men were traveling together before chancing upon April and her family, they would not remain separated for long. If April was injured too badly to walk, the men had probably seen the canoe as the only option for taking her with them, and it was feasible to do so only because they were headed downstream anyway. They couldn't all go in the boat of course, but if one of them had taken it with her and Kimberly aboard, it was likely they planned to rendezvous soon, probably before dark so they could camp together. If that were the case, then following the trail of these three would lead him to her anyway. Trying to catch up with the canoe might not be so easy. He didn't know if any of these men had experience with canoes, but he did know that a skilled paddler could get down the creek much faster than anyone hiking at a normal pace on foot. This was mainly because it was impossible to follow the waterway bend-for-bend, making walking slow and difficult, while the current in the creek would assist even a casual paddler in making good time.

He had no idea where they were going or how far they intended to travel, but Mitch knew if he were to have any hope of catching up, he was going to have to move and move fast. He could follow the three on foot without much difficulty and if he was right, they would rejoin the one who had paddled off with April and Kimberly. But if he was wrong and they didn't have plans to meet up somewhere downstream, then he would have no way of knowing where or how far the one in the canoe was taking her. Catching up to the other three and taking them out would be easy enough, but if they did not rendezvous with the canoe, he was going to have to take at least one of them alive to find out their intended destination. It was a risk, but Mitch decided the risk of not being able to catch up to the canoe was greater. He needed to stick to the trail of the three because that was a trail he could follow. If they didn't lead him to April and Kimberly directly, he was determined to make them do so by whatever means necessary. And if he had to follow Black Creek all the way to the Pascagoula River and beyond to find them, he would do that too.

Eighteen

JASON BURNS STOOD WATCHING until Mitch disappeared into the woods on the opposite side of Black Creek, then he set out to make his way back to the Henley farm and house. The trail they had been following since Mitch had found the spot where one of them hit the deer with the arrow had led them quite far from home this morning. Jason was familiar with the woods in the immediate vicinity of the farm, but every time he followed Mitch farther afield on a hunt, he realized just how vast these river land forests really were. He hoped he could find his way back without too much difficulty, but he would have preferred not to have to do it alone. Mitch was depending on him though, so he was determined to get there as soon as he could. He had to let Lisa and the others know what was going on and just as importantly, get them to come back with him for David.

Jason had checked one last time before he left to make sure the unconscious man was still breathing and that he still had a pulse. Nothing had changed in that regard but he still showed no signs of coming to, so there was nothing more he could do by himself. A part of him wished he was going with

Mitch instead, tracking down the men who took April. Jason barely knew her, but he felt like he owed her a lot. First, she had helped Mitch get him back to the house after the two of them found him beaten half to death on the side of the road. Then she'd risked her life to help Mitch rescue his little sister Stacy, who along with Mitch's sister Lisa, was in the hands of those worthless Wallace brothers who'd done that to him and left him for dead. After that, she had fought fearlessly by Mitch's side when they were attacked in Hattiesburg, helping Mitch defeat a gang of looters. From everything Mitch had told him about their journey together, Jason knew April was really something special.

Jason was so out of it when he met her that he couldn't remember many details of her face or her voice. But Mitch had been infatuated with her and even all these months afterwards; she frequently came up in conversation. Jason knew it had to be an incredible shock for Mitch to see her again today, especially out here in these woods after all this time. And it had to be much more of a shock to see her in such a dangerous predicament. If Mitch had asked him to, Jason would have certainly gone with him to help find her, not only for his sake but for what she had done for him and Stacy as well. But despite this sense of obligation, another part of him was also relieved that Mitch sent him on this other, far less dangerous task.

Perhaps he had in him a bit of cowardice; Jason was not afraid to admit, at least to himself. But he didn't relish the idea of trying to track down four heavily armed men with the intention of taking their prize away from them. It had been one thing this morning, tracking the unknown lone hunter with Mitch, who was leading the way and knew exactly what to do. Jason hadn't expected that they would have trouble, but if they did, he had confidence in Mitch and the numbers were two to one in their favor. But when that one had turned into four, and the four had proven what they were capable of and willing to do, the picture was suddenly different. There could only be one thing at the end of the trail Mitch was following—and that was a fight—almost certainly a fight that would end in death for the loser.

Jason knew fighting for survival was a part of the new reality they all found themselves in, but still, he didn't like it. He was doing better than before, without a doubt, but he had a long way to go yet and knew he would likely never be even half as competent as Mitch. Adapting to a life without cars and electricity was hard enough. But then he had to learn how to hunt and kill animals just to eat. Hunting and woodcraft were things Jason had no interest in before the grid went down, despite the fact that he lived in a small community practically surrounded by national forest lands. Most of the other guys he went to school with had grown up hunting squirrels, deer and other game with their fathers and brothers, but Jason had neither of those to take him or teach him how. He and Stacy lived with their mom and only saw their dad for a couple of weeks in the summer, when they went to visit him and their stepmother at his home in Dallas.

Jason's only passion before the pulse shut down the power grid was music, and he spent most of his spare time after school locked in his room with his guitar and amp. Though it was only a cheaper, imported imitation of the Fender Stratocaster he dreamed of, Jason learned to play it and play it well. He had been determined to get as good as the rock stars he idolized when he suddenly found himself unplugged by the effects of the solar flare.

Weeks later, after he was healed from his injuries and he and Stacy still had not heard from their mother, Jason and Mitch had made the journey back to the little town of Brooklyn on foot. Following the Black Creek hiking trail that roughly paralleled the stream, they went back that last time to see if his mom had somehow made it back home, but found no sign that she had. To this day Jason did not know if she was alive or dead, but he had come to accept the greater likelihood of the latter possibility. They had taken a few things from the house, and though it was a burden, Jason shouldered the guitar as well and carried it back to the Henley farm. He still picked it up now and then, even though it would never sound the same without the amplifier and his effects pedals and he sometimes wondered why he bothered. It didn't look like the lights were ever going to come back on again, and his dream of someday playing on stage in front of his screaming fans seemed farther away than it ever had.

Now instead of learning new lead riffs, he was studying

the habits of game animals and learning to move quietly through the woods. Under Mitch's tutorage, he was slowly getting more proficient at shooting guns and even the bow and arrow. He had made a few kills of his own; although Mitch brought home far more of the meat they needed than anyone else staying at the house. Mitch had shown him how to skin an animal and gut it, and though he still hated the feel of the slimy entrails and warm blood on his hands, he could do a passible job with everything from a rabbit to a whitetail buck. It no longer bothered him to kill, but so far he had avoided having to kill another human being—something Mitch had done numerous times since the blackout. Jason had no doubt he would be doing it again soon too, he just hoped his friend could indeed maintain the element of surprise that he so badly needed in his favor. If things went as he expected, he would soon be coming back home and bringing April and her little girl with him.

"I sure wish he would have waited for the rest of us!" Lisa said when Jason finally made it back and told her where her brother had gone. "He's so nuts about April he just couldn't wait. He's always taking chances he shouldn't, and it really worries me."

"He didn't want them to get that much of a head start," Jason said. "He said he didn't even want to let them out of his sight long enough to come find me, but he knew he had to. It would have taken way to long to come all the way back here first, especially if we were trying to bring David back on

141

a travois."

"It's still stupid for him to take off tracking four men by himself. I think we need to follow that trail too, just in case he's in trouble and needs help. We could all go back to the creek together, and Stacy, Corey and Samantha could get David moved back here. You and I could go after Mitch. I've been shot at before. I'm not afraid."

"Yeah but what if we can't follow the trail? No one can track people and animals like Mitch. And what if we make too much noise and mess up his plans? We could make it worse, and besides, by the time we even get there, I'll bet he will have already caught those guys and taken them out. He might have already done it now."

Lisa continued to argue but Jason cut her off. "Let's just get back to the creek first and then decide. That David guy is lying out there in the woods unconscious and helpless. Anything could come along and find him, and he *is* April's husband. She probably thinks he's dead. It will be a nice surprise for her when Mitch does bring her and Kimberly back and he's here waiting for them. If he ever wakes up, that is."

Lisa agreed that whatever they were going to do, they couldn't waste time. She went to her room and got her rifle and Stacy's and then made sure Corey and Samantha were armed too; Corey with a shotgun and Samantha with a 10/22 carbine. Jason wasn't sure how those two would react if they got into a gunfight, but it made sense for them to at least carry weapons. Corey and Samantha had less experience with guns and the woods than Jason did before the pulse, if that were even possible. Refugees from the Gulf coast town of Long Beach, these two nineteen-year-old college students had turned up at the farm about a month ago after escaping from a shelter that had turned out to be more of a prison than a safe haven. Though they hadn't known each other before the collapse, they were a devoted couple by the time they got to the Henley property. Mitch had liked both of them from the start, and seeing that they were not a threat and could possibly be an asset on the property, he had taken them in with the consent of the others. It never hurt to have more eyes and more guns to keep watch over the house and farm when he was away, and though they were unskilled when they arrived, both were eager to learn how to hunt and willing to work and do whatever else was needed to earn their place there.

Jason didn't like leaving the house unguarded now, and he knew Mitch wouldn't either, but he was afraid he wouldn't be able to stop Lisa from taking off after Mitch even if he didn't agree to go and if she did, he would need all the help he could get dragging a travois all the way back here through the woods. Even if Lisa was reasonable and decided to come back with them it would be good to have extra help, so they all set off together, with him leading the way.

He didn't have much trouble finding his way back after having just come from the place across the creek from the sandbar where April and Kimberly were taken. But when they arrived on the wooded bank and he confirmed it was the right place, David was nowhere to be seen. He was not where he and Mitch had left him, lying in the shade of a giant white oak, nor was he anywhere nearby as far as Jason could see.

"He's gone!" Jason said, turning around to look at Lisa and the others with disbelief.

"Are you sure this is the right place?" Lisa asked.

"Yes, there's no doubt in my mind. He was right here under this tree. And look, right over there across the creek; that's the sandbar where Mitch saw those guys knock him out and kidnapped April and her baby. I was over there with him. We carried David across the river and put him here. He was still out cold when I left. That couldn't have been more than about an hour and a half ago."

"Yeah, I believe you," Lisa said. "She was down on her knees examining the compressed leaves where the weight of David's body had been. Jason knew that while she wasn't nearly the tracker her brother was, she did know a whole lot more about it than he did.

"Do you think something got him?" Jason asked. "Mitch said the wild dogs and coyotes would find him if we left him out here at night, but it's still a couple of hours before dark."

"I don't see any blood or drag marks, but I'm looking. Just give me a few minutes. There's got to be an explanation for this."

Nineteen

WHEN HE OPENED HIS eyes he saw a tall canopy of leafy treetops far overhead, obscuring most of the sky except for a few patches of blue in the gaps between the branches. Floating across those patches of sky were a few puffy cumulous clouds, drifting slowly to the south, pushed by the north wind that chilled the air just enough to make him slightly uncomfortable. The view of clouds, sky and trees was confusing but almost hypnotic. He continued to stare at it for what seemed like quite a long time, with little desire to move or look elsewhere.

With the realization that what he was seeing was real, there came another sensation of dull, throbbing pain from the left side of his head. The pain was getting worse, or at least he was becoming more aware of it, making it seem so. It felt like a deep ache, radiating from inside his skull to the contact point on the ground beneath his head, making him want to lift it up to make it stop. But when he tried to sit up, it seemed to get worse. He reached up with his left hand to touch the area that was the source of the pain and felt a lump beneath his fingers. Pressing on it made the hurt more intense, so he drew his hand away. Keeping his head as still as possible, he rolled his eyes from side-to-side to try and determine where he was. All he saw was trees. There was nothing surrounding him but trees and the deep litter of leaves and pine straw that covered the ground where he lay on the forest floor.

In addition to the rustle of wind through the leafy canopy overhead, he heard the chirps and singing of small birds hidden in the foliage somewhere nearby. But there was another sound too that seemed to come from somewhere out there among the trees. It was constant and melodic, a gentle sound that at first he did not recognize and that made no sense. Once again, he attempted to lift his head, and this time he pushed through the pain, rolling onto his side to lift his body up on one elbow so that he could look in the direction of that mysterious sound. What he saw glimmering through the foliage down the slope beneath him explained it. It was the sound of running water; the gentle flowing of a river or stream. He could see the current swirling as it parted around a protruding stump a short distance from the bank, the rush of its movement contributing to the music the river played.

Farther out, on the other side of the moving water, was a shimmering beach of white sand, standing out in stark contrast to the deep green of the forest and the dark water that bordered it. He stared at it for several more minutes, propped on his elbow as he took in the surroundings and tried to remember where he was. He didn't have a clue how he got here and why he awoke alone in this place. The pain in his head came and went in throbbing waves, making it hard to think of anything else, much less concentrate or remember. He didn't know why it was hurting so, or what caused the knot that seemed to be the source. He had no memory of falling and hitting his head, but he figured that must have been what happened.

Thinking of this, he realized he couldn't remember where he was supposed to be either, much less how he'd gotten to such a beautiful place and why he'd come. He looked down at his feet and saw the worn leather of the Timberland hiking boots he was wearing. Those were familiar, and seemed to belong there. He always wore those boots, he could remember that for sure. The faded Levis covering his legs felt natural as well, as did the gray sweatshirt that was barely warm enough now that the afternoon sun was filtering through the trees at a low angle. He figured he must have taken a nap, and that he had slept much later than he planned to. Whatever the reason, he knew he couldn't lie there like that any longer. He had to get somewhere important, he just couldn't remember where it was or why.

Ignoring the agony of his headache, he rolled the rest of the way from where he was propped on his elbow until he was on his hands and knees. Unable to move further until the waves of pain subsided again, he paused in that position, staring down at the leaves between his hands, watching a trickling stream of tiny ants that were clearly on their way to somewhere important too. Knowing he had to get moving just like them, he watched for a few more minutes before pushing himself up into a kneeling position. His hands free again, he reached up once more to touch the knot on his head. It felt huge, and he wished he had a mirror so he could see. Whatever he had hit his head against, it must have been a hard lick. He wondered if anyone had been with him when it happened, but then he figured probably not. If he was alone here now, he must have been alone then too. He couldn't think of anyone who would have been with him anyway. In fact, he couldn't think of anyone at all and wasn't sure if he had seen any other people in a long time. If he was here in these woods alone now, maybe he had been here longer than he could remember, but surely not in this spot, because the stream and the sandy beach did not look familiar. He didn't recognize it so it couldn't be the right place. Grabbing ahold of the trunk of a small sapling for support, he pulled himself the rest of the way to his feet, thinking maybe it would come to him if he could get a better view and have a look around.

He felt dizzy when his full weight was on his feet, but the sensation gradually subsided and he began walking around in circles, looking for some clue as to where to go or what to do next. The answer didn't come to him yet, but he became aware of his thirst and of his hunger. The first was easy to satisfy. He made his way down the bank and knelt at the edge of the stream. The water was dark, like the color of aged whiskey, but even so it was clear and not clouded with mud.

It was cold and when he dipped up a double handful to his lips it tasted good. He drank his fill and splashed the cold water on the lump on the side of his head. It gave him some temporary relief but the aching inside his skull did not go away.

As he knelt there, he saw schools of minnows darting about around submerged branches and the water plants growing in the shallows. He was really hungry and the tiny fish looked irresistible. He plunged into the creek grabbing at them with both hands, but even though he felt one in his grasp more than once, they slipped between his fingers before he could close his fists. It didn't matter though, because the cold water felt good to him, despite the cool temperature of the air. He dunked his head under and at last got some relief from his headache. Pushing off with his feet, he swam into the main channel and rolled onto his back, floating, allowing the current to carry him downstream. It felt so good that he continued to drift; alternating swimming and floating until he finally started feeling too cold to stay in any longer.

The sandbar was out of sight now, around the bend upstream, but across the creek on the same side, there was an opening in the dense woods that looked enticing. He swam across until his feet touched bottom and waded out of the water on the other side. The opening was a dry streambed, with steep clay banks from the top of which tall leaning trees closed overhead. He walked into the entrance, finding a natural path in the muddy bottom of the ditch. Looking down in the mixed sand and mud, he saw that there were other footprints everywhere. The footprints puzzled him, but he knew they had to mean he was in the right place. Other people lived around here for sure, and if they did, they probably had food. All he had to do was keep walking up this ditch until he found them. He forgot about his pain as he started out, picking his way along the bottom of the winding ditch with growing anticipation of what he was sure he would soon find.

Twenty

THE SUDDEN BOOM OF a nearby gunshot echoed through the woods from somewhere ahead; somewhere around the next bend in the river. April saw the surprise in Wayne's eyes as he stopped talking mid-sentence and kept his paddle in the water mid-stroke, using the blade as a steering oar as he let the boat drift.

"That was a shotgun!" he whispered. "Don't move, and don't make a sound!"

April had not been talking anyway. She had been holding Kimberly close, ignoring his incessant chatter as she gently rocked her baby and whispered in her ear. All she had wanted was for him to shut up and leave her alone. It was bad enough that she was sitting there tied in the canoe, facing him, his eyes upon her the entire time while he paddled downstream.

But he hadn't stopped talking until now. It was obvious that he had not seen a woman for weeks, if not months, much less talked to one, and that he was not going to shut up, either now or when they got to where he was taking her. He claimed that the camp where they were going was on land he and the others with him had purchased long before the blackout, a hunting club of some kind, and that they had it well stocked for long-term self-sufficiency. That was why even after all these months they still had enough of the MREs they carried to go off on this long-range hunting and scouting trip without having to actually hunt for food.

April was grateful for the peanut butter in the one he gave her that she fed to Kimberly, but she had no appetite herself right now. She knew she would have to eat what they offered her as time went on, but right now she was so angry and so sick with fear for her child and disgusted at what they had done to David that she wanted nothing to do with food.

Ever since they had started downstream in the canoe, her mind had raced with thoughts of escaping this deranged maniac and she was desperate to come up with a way to do so before he rejoined the other three. If it seemed hopeless now, she knew it would be even worse when there were four of them again, especially with Kimberly to worry about. But even if she did not have her child to carry, she couldn't run and could hardly walk. The swelling of her ankle had gotten worse since she'd been sitting in the canoe, and she knew she could barely put any weight on it when she stood.

The shotgun blast coming from so close and in the direction they were headed was clearly a surprise to Wayne, because it meant someone they didn't know about was in the immediate area. He said that it was for sure a shotgun and that you could tell by the dull booming report that was quite different from the crack of a high-powered rifle. April knew that was why it alarmed him. None of the others with him had been carrying a shotgun. They were all armed with military-style carbines of the AK and AR variety, though Wayne himself was carrying only a compound bow and the Glock pistol he wore in a low-slung holster.

Kimberly had finally fallen asleep in her arms until the loud noise of the gun going off caused her to stir. April knew even before Wayne warned her with a stern whisper that she'd better keep her child quiet. He was clearly upset that there was an armed stranger so close by, and he would probably do anything to make sure neither her or Kimberly made a sound that might give away their presence on the creek.

Without taking the blade out of the water, he steered the canoe with the paddle until it brushed up against a steep clay bank that was overhung with low branches and vines. He tied the bow painter to an exposed root and then sat there in silence, waiting and listening.

"It's probably someone hunting," he whispered, "but I'm not paddling around that bend out in the open in the middle of this creek. Whoever it is could be right on the bank downstream. I'm going to slip down there on foot and have a look. You're going to sit here and keep that kid quiet and not make a sound, do you understand?"

April's ankles were already tied together but before Wayne climbed up to the top of the bank, he bound her wrists again, but in a way so that she could still hold Kimberly and keep her quiet. He then and secured one end of a piece of the long line that was looped around her neck to an overhanging branch once he gained the top of the bank. In this position, there was no way she could struggle to work her bindings loose without fear of capsize. She looked at the fast-moving water rushing under the canoe against the bank and it made her nervous. She knew the deepest channels always ran up against the outside banks of the creek's bends, and in many of these places there were eddies and other confused currents.

"The canoe could flip over here," she whispered. " I will be hung and Kimberly will drown if it does!"

"You're exactly right. But if you sit still and don't move, that won't happen. So sit still!" he whispered back. "I'm not taking this canoe one bit farther down this creek until I find whoever fired that shotgun. It's not worth the risk of getting ambushed. I don't expect this to take long, because whoever fired that shotgun was really close."

* * *

Wayne Parker looked at April and her baby one more time from atop the bank above the canoe. The clever way he'd devised to tie her neck to the branch high above her assured him she wasn't going anywhere until he returned. He didn't have to worry about her trying anything stupid; if she made a wrong move, it would indeed flip over and they would both be dead. The boat was well hidden, tied there under those overhanging bushes, and the current she had been worried about indeed made getting in and out of it without capsizing tricky. He had pulled himself up using roots sticking out of the bank, his bow slung over his back until he reached the top.

Wayne didn't want to come back and find them dead, but he was sure April had enough sense not to try and escape. He didn't want to leave her at all, but this sudden shotgun blast really had him concerned. He and the others had seen no one on their trek upstream from their camp until they stumbled upon April and her family. Whoever fired that shotgun may have been in the vicinity then too, but if so, they had not seen or heard any sign of them.

Before he set out to investigate, he unholstered the Glock 20 he wore on his right thigh and double-checked to make sure there was a round in the chamber. He already knew there was without looking, but it just made him feel better to verify it again anyway. Carrying a pistol like that was what gave him the confidence to travel with his bow as his only other weapon. There was nothing that walked in these woods that the 10mm couldn't take down, and with the Glock Model 20's 15-round capacity, he felt little need to be burdened by a rifle as well. It was nice to know it was on his side and ready for action, but the bow was what he would carry at ready, and he withdrew a carbon-fiber shaft with a Wasp Sharpshooter broadhead screwed on the tip and started in the direction from which gunshot came.

Creeping through the creek-side undergrowth, he stayed as close to the bank as the vegetation allowed. The sound of the shotgun was loud enough that he knew whoever fired it could not be far away, because it would not carry near as far as a rifle report. He planned to check out the area around the next bend that had been out of sight from where they were when they heard it, and if there was nothing there, he would check out at least one more. He had to make sure that whoever was around was not waiting right there on the bank when they continued downstream in the canoe.

Wayne was furious at the delay but there was nothing else he could do but stop and check out the situation. There was no other way to get to the planned rendezvous with Gary and the others than to continue down Black Creek. April's ankle had gotten worse and he wasn't leaving her behind after all this. If there was somebody standing between him and getting her back to the camp like he planned, then it was just simply going to be that person's unlucky day. For whatever reason they did it, shooting that shotgun came at just the right time to prevent Wayne from paddling blindly into view with his two captives. He would have literally been a sitting duck out there in the middle of the creek for someone to take a potshot at and he had little doubt that they would do it to. Wayne Parker didn't trust anyone these days, and he intended to be the one who got the chance to shoot first now.

His guess that whoever it was couldn't be far away seemed confirmed when he heard a faint clank of metal on metal. There was nothing in nature that made a sound like that. Woodpeckers might sound like a man chopping wood or hammering nails, but no animal or bird banged metal against metal. He locked the mechanical release onto his bowstring and held the weapon at ready as he crept forward with more caution. The sound continued and he had no doubt that someone was just ahead, probably the same person who fired the shotgun. The only reason he couldn't already see them was because of undergrowth.

He crept closer, holding the bow at ready in front of him until he came within view of an open area just downstream on the bank that looked like a place that had been frequently used as a campsite, probably long before the blackout. It was shaded by tall trees like those of the rest of the forest, but the understory of bushes and other vegetation had been cleared away and the ground was mostly bare earth. Pulled up from the creek's edge was a green canoe, not aluminum like the one he had been paddling with April and Kimberly, but instead made of some kind of plastic or fiberglass. Beside it, a longhaired man was kneeling on the ground, carefully rolling up what appeared to be a big tent that he had just taken down. A pile of aluminum poles and metal tent stakes was stacked beside it. Wayne surmised that the clanking sound he'd heard was probably the sound of the man banging the tent stakes together to knock the dirt off of them before packing them away. He scanned the campsite area for any sign of a shotgun but did not see one. If this was the man who'd just fired one, and Wayne had no doubt that he was, it was probably lying close by but behind the tent or something where he couldn't see it from this angle. The good thing was that as the man worked at rolling the tent into as tight a package as possible, his back was turned to him. Wayne was able to slip in closer without making a sound once he stepped into the park-like opening.

Wayne didn't care what the man was doing there or what his story was. He looked rough and outdoorsy, as if he had been living in the woods out here ever since the blackout occurred. For a moment, he wondered if this man could be the "friend" April mentioned that lived near here. Whether he was or not, it didn't matter. The man and his canoe were between him and where he needed to be that night. Even if he was ready to leave now and was shoving his boat in the water, he would be a problem, because he would be just ahead of them. They would run the risk of either overtaking him on the creek or catching up the first time he stopped for some reason. Wayne wasn't into running unnecessary risks. The range from where he stood now was no more than forty yards. He drew the bow and put the sight in the center of the man's back.

Just as he pressed the release to let his carbon fiber missile fly downrange to its target, a terrifying and unmistakable sound from off in the bushes to his right caused

158

him to flinch. He heard his arrow strike flesh but because he was so startled his bow arm jerked at the last second. He saw the bright vanes of the fletching disappear not into his intended target, but instead into the back of the man's arm just before he turned to face whoever it was that had racked the slide of a pump-action shotgun. There was no time to draw another arrow or even think about reaching for the Glock. A white-bearded man with wild gray hair as long as the other man's already had a bead on him at point-blank range. Wayne Parker didn't even get a chance to speak. The last thing he was aware of before the old man pulled the trigger was just how big the gaping black hole that was the business end of a 12-gauge shotgun looked from just ten feet away.

Twenty-one

MITCH STOPPED IN HIS tracks at the sound of a gunshot from somewhere off in the distance in the general direction he was headed. He knew immediately that it was the blast of a shotgun rather than the crack of a high-powered assault rifle like those the four men who took April were carrying. He had not seen any shotguns at all and the two weapons they took from April and David were both rifles. That didn't rule out the possibility that one of them had a takedown shotgun in his backpack, but Mitch figured it was more likely that someone else fired the shot. He stood still and listened, waiting to see if there would be a follow-up shot or possible return fire from another weapon, but even after a good three or four minutes, there was nothing.

Despite the fact that the sound had come from some distance downstream, where the men he was following were likely to be, Mitch knew the gunshot could be unrelated to them. There was always the possibility of other survivors in the vicinity of the creek, and shotguns were a natural choice for hunting most of the available game in these woods. But even if it was someone unrelated to the four who took April and Kimberly, Mitch was sure that they must have heard the blast too. From where they were, the shooter had to be closer to them than to him.

He picked up the pace a bit as he got moving again. It would not bode well for April and her little girl if the one paddling the canoe got into an encounter with other strangers. He hoped something like that wouldn't happen, but the sooner he closed in on the three he was following the better. He wanted to catch up and be there watching when they met the canoe, wherever that might be, especially since the coming darkness after they made camp would likely provide his best opportunity for a swift rescue.

The trail of the three soon led to the edge of a wide slough of stagnant brown water and Mitch followed their tracks where they tried to find a way around it. He knew they wouldn't have been able to though, unless they wanted to go a half-mile out of their way. The slough was typical of the many that connected to Black Creek in this area, and he knew that the farther downstream one traveled, the more numerous they were as the land became more low-lying and swampy near the creek's end.

The sloughs and swamps were usually shallow though, most of them full of cypress and other water-tolerant trees that grew right in the middle of them. Mitch soon found the place where the men had given up on going around and had finally waded right in. It was the only sensible thing to do if one were to attempt to follow the watercourse without

162

making ridiculously long detours.

It was about a hundred feet across to the other side, and though his feet sank a few inches into the muddy bottom in some places, Mitch didn't get wet above mid-thigh even in the deepest part. When he reached the opposite bank, he had to side step to avoid a big cottonmouth, which was not an unexpected encounter along the edges of waters like this, despite the cooler fall weather. The big snake was coiled around a protruding cypress knee, eyeing him intently, but Mitch didn't get close enough to give it any reason to feel threatened and turn aggressive. He searched the mud on the other side until he found the place where the three men had exited the water earlier, and had just started tracking again when another gun blast just like the first echoed through the trees from the same direction.

He stopped again and waited. Two widely spaced shots like that could be explained by any number of things, and was certainly not out of the ordinary for hunters. The second shot coming some 15 or 20 minutes later could have been fired to finish off a deer or other game animal wounded by the first and then tracked down. Or, if the hunter was after small game such as squirrels, it could mean he or she made a second kill after the first. Mitch wouldn't have given it much thought any other time; it was just that it had to be happening so close to those he sought. When there was no third blast from the shotgun and still no answer from a different weapon, he just shrugged and got moving again, threading his way along the easy trail the three men left, but staying alert and pausing often to listen as he went.

* * *

Gary Haggard froze and raised a hand in an unmistakable gesture that was a signal to "halt" to his two buddies that were right behind him. The shotgun blast from somewhere to the southeast, in the general direction of the creek was sudden and completely unexpected. Would there be another one? Would he hear Wayne's 10mm Glock return fire? Did the shooter even know Wayne and the woman and kid were in the vicinity? Gary didn't know, but he did know that it meant someone else was out here and that they were armed.

He and Jared and Paul were in one of those places where their path had taken them quite far from the creek bank. They had already waded three sloughs and were soaked to the waist, and a huge area of hurricane-damaged forest that was now overgrown in thickets had forced them to veer on quite a wide detour to the north. He didn't like being this far away from the creek; for one thing, it was too easy to get disoriented in these bottomland forests and lose a lot of time just navigating. For another, he worried about just such an event as what could have just happened. Had some local woodsman hiding on the bank taken a potshot at Wayne as he paddled past? Gary wouldn't be surprised. People tended to shoot first and ask questions later these days, and there was no law answer to anywhere anyway, especially way out here where no one would even know.

"What do you think?" Jared whispered.

"I don't know. I just know it proves somebody else is out here besides us. And they've got a shotgun."

"Do you think the woman was telling the truth?" Paul asked. "That maybe there really were more people traveling with them, in other canoes?"

"I guess it's possible, but I doubt it. Why wouldn't they all stay together if they were doing that? It would be stupid to split up and divide your forces these days, considering what all could happen."

"Yeah, just like you tried to tell Wayne this morning."

"Exactly! Anyway, I think she was lying; hoping we would be afraid of her imaginary friends and leave the three of them alone. I suspect that whoever fired that shotgun is some local yokel that lives out here somewhere. I just hope he wasn't shooting at Wayne. We'd better try to work our way closer to the creek bank, just in case. I don't like this being separated one bit, but Wayne's got some fantasy about taming that girl and keeping her around. You can't tell him a damned thing!"

They still weren't past the blow-down area, so getting to the creek bank was not going to be easy. The briar patches and tangles of bushes were almost impenetrable in places, forcing Gary to use the machete more than he would like, but he was careful to cut as quietly as possible. They had traversed maybe a hundred yards of this when a second

165

gunshot rang out, sounding just like the first.

"Same shotgun!" Gary whispered.

"It sounded to me like it came from about the same place as the first one," Jared said.

"Yeah, I think you're right. I still think it's near the creek too, but no telling whether whoever it is upstream or downstream of where Wayne is by now. We need to get closer and try to reach the bank and stick to it until we find him. I don't like this at all. All he's got is that damned bow and his Glock. Somebody with a twelve-gauge loaded with slugs or double-ought buck would have him at a disadvantage, even with the 10mm."

"Yeah, especially with him sitting out there in the open in that canoe," Paul said.

"Let's keep moving. Whatever's going on over there on the creek, the sooner we get there, the better. But we've got to stay alert and be careful. There's no way to tell at this point whether that shotgunner is on our side of the creek or the other side. We'll just have to deal with these briars and stuff. Can't risk using the blade any more because there could be others in the area that could hear us coming and set up an ambush."

Twenty-two

APRIL WAS IMMENSELY RELIEVED when Wayne climbed out of the canoe and disappeared into the woods out of her sight downstream. As helpless as she and Kimberly were, tied in that narrow canoe in a dangerous patch of swift current under a steep clay bank; at least he was gone! She felt like she could breath freely again for the first time since the men had walked into their camp this morning. She was sick of looking at him and sick of hearing him talk. Though he had kept his voice low so it wouldn't carry far, he had not stopped running his mouth since they embarked in the canoe. It had been difficult for her to even think clearly as long as he was bothering her with his constant barrage of questions and comments.

Kimberly was finally sleeping again too, worn out as she was by all the action and the upset that had her crying with fear, frustration and exhaustion most of the day. April sat there staring at her as she held her close, almost afraid to move for fear of rolling the canoe upside down. If that happened, her baby would drown with no one there to right it. And she would be hanging by her neck, probably still alive long enough to know it was her fault Kimberly drowned because of her upsetting the boat. Despite the risks, however, April knew she had to think of a way out of this situation. With Wayne out of sight, now might be the only chance she would ever get to try and escape, but how was it even possible? His last minute idea of securing the other end of the rope about her neck to an overhanging branch once he climbed up there had been good thinking on his part.

She couldn't pull herself up by the line, because of the way her wrists and ankles were bound and secured to the seat upon which she sat. This left her no way of relieving any tension on the overhead line, so she had little hope of working the knots around her ankles loose or slipping her wrists free. Any pulling or struggle with enough effort to make a difference would surely capsize the boat. All she could do was sit there in helpless frustration as the minutes ticked by, knowing Wayne would soon be back and her opportunity would be gone.

She stared at the bank beside her as she thought and waited. A thick matt of bright green moss with clumps of small ferns growing out of it covered much of the near vertical clay wall. Long, stringy roots from the trees growing on top hung like vines down the side too, exposed by times of high water, when the creek washed away the soil surrounding them. In time the bank would erode further, sending the trees on top crashing into the creek, obstructing the channel like so many others that anyone paddling its current had to navigate around. Looking closer at the bank, she saw that its walls were home to all sorts of small creatures: ants, spiders and large beetles she did not recognize. She began to worry about wasps and bees, or maybe even a snake. What would she do if a snake fell into the canoe with her and Kimberly? She hated being in such a helpless situation. But she was going to hate it worse when Wayne came back.

If only her memory had been better, the two of them wouldn't be in the predicament. She was sure that she and David must have somehow missed the correct sandbar and the path that led to Mitch Henley's property. It was her fault for being such an incompetent navigator. She was such a city girl, even now after spending that time in the woods with Mitch. She should have been able to spot the trail and if she had, they would be all be safe on the Henley farm by now. She could do little else, so beating herself up for her own inadequacies was as good as anything. What would become of her precious Kimberly now because of her failure?

The sudden report of another shotgun blast snapped her out of these thoughts and woke Kimberly from her short nap. April whispered to her, trying to reassure her when she started crying, but with her hands tied the way they were, she couldn't give her the mother's touch that would make the difference. Kimberly only got more agitated, and April could do nothing to quiet her.

She didn't know what this second shot meant. It was

quite close, of that she was certain, and it was indeed in the downstream direction just like the first one; the same way that Wayne had gone. He had to be much closer to whoever fired it than she was. So what had happened? Was someone shooting at him? He had not fired his pistol, but he could have used his bow and she wouldn't have known. April could do nothing but wait, and the not knowing would make the minutes pass like hours.

* * *

Benny Evans racked the slide of his Savage Model 30 12-gauge pump to chamber another round while keeping an eye on the fallen man. He saw that he wouldn't need it as he stepped closer. The stranger's legs were still kicking in involuntary spasms, but that would be over in a few seconds. He had only been some twenty paces away when he shot him squarely in the chest. The double-ought buckshot had made quite a mess at that range, and he wouldn't need to waste another shell.

He rushed passed the body in a hurry to check on his boy. He knew Tommy had been hit and he wasn't sure where, but at least he was still alive—for now. He was on his knees next to the tent he'd been packing, doubled over and clutching at his upper arm. When Benny reached his side, there was blood everywhere, streaming down the wounded arm and covering his son's other hand that he was using to try and stop the flow. Tommy was in so much distress and pain he wasn't even aware of his approach until Benny knelt beside him.

"My arm! What hit me, Pop?"

Benny saw that there was no arrow lodged in the arm or even in sight. The high-powered bow had sent it through his boy's arm and it still went flying somewhere, probably to bury under the thick leaves all around them on the ground. At least that meant that it had missed the bone in his upper arm, and that was good. There would be no broadhead to dig out, but he had to get the bleeding stopped before his boy bled to death. Benny laid the shotgun down and stripped off his belt. He passed it around Tommy's shoulder and armpit and pulled it tight.

"It was an arrow, son. That fellow shot you with a damned arrow. It was the last one he'll ever shoot though, I'll tell you that!"

"Who was it? Where'd he come from? I didn't see nobody. Didn't hear nobody either."

"I know. He just slipped right up here from somewhere upstream. It was just luck that I was almost back here when I saw him draw down on you. I didn't have round in the chamber because I'd just killed a hen turkey over there on the other side of the hollow. He heard me rack the slide and I think it caused him to jump a little. Otherwise, he might have got you right in the middle of the back."

Tommy was in a lot of pain. With the bleeding slowed,

Benny was able to wipe away enough blood to see what kind of damage had been done. The broadhead had sliced through the triceps area and had probably done a lot damage to both muscles and nerves. But it didn't hit an artery; otherwise Tommy might not make it.

"You're gonna be all right, son. You're lucky though!"

"Are you sure he was by himself," Tommy asked, as he finally looked up and over in the direction of the fallen bowman.

"As far as I know he was. But he wasn't carrying any gear. I'm thinking he didn't walk way out here with nothing on him. I'm wondering if he ain't got a boat or something upstream. I'm gonna have a look as soon as I get you situated and make sure you're not gonna bleed out, son."

"I'm all right. You'd better go have a look around."

"I'm gonna make a bandage that'll put some pressure on that wound. Since that arrow didn't cut an artery, I can get that belt off so you don't lose your arm. You're gonna have a long go of healing though, the way it cut through the muscles. I just hope you can get your strength back."

"I'll be fine. I'm just glad you got him."

"Me too. Anybody that would try to kill you just like that for no reason at all, ain't no telling what he was up to or what he had done before. If anybody *is* with him, they'll likely be just as bad."

"That's why you need to go find out now, Pop. You can make a better bandage when you get back. Just give me my

172

spare shirt out of pack over there and I'll keep the pressure on it myself."

Benny knew his boy was right. If there was anybody else out here that had been traveling with that fellow, Benny needed to find them and deal with them now. Both of them got lucky this time. If he had been just a minute later returning with that turkey, Tommy would be dead. And the killer would have taken him out too if he had half a chance. If he had, it would have been a mercy. Benny wouldn't have known what to do if he lost Tommy too. His forty-year-old son was all he had left in this world that he cared about, and besides, without his help, he knew he wouldn't be able to make it out here alone. Not at his age.

Once he made sure Tommy could hold the pressure on his wound so he wouldn't lose any more blood, Benny started up the creek, slipping quietly into the underbrush in the direction the man had come from. He stepped carefully and kept his eyes and ears open, the Savage pump chambered and fully loaded in his hands, the barrel out front and at the ready as he stalked. He knew he couldn't take a chance, and if he saw anything move he intended to open up on it. Considering what that fellow had done, there wasn't any sense waiting to see.

He'd made it to the end of the next bend upstream and still there was no sign of anyone. He was about to turn around and go back to see about his boy, deciding that the man must have been alone after all when he heard something coming from the direction of the creek. There was a steep bank off to his right, and he couldn't see the water at its base from where he stood listening. At first, he thought it might be some strange trick of the water, a gurgling or bubbling of current, but the more he listened, the more he was sure that wasn't it. It was a baby crying, clear as could be. There was no doubt about it. Benny's grip tensed on the shotgun stock and he crept to the bank as quietly as possibly, keeping it pointed ahead and ready to shoot as he made his way to the edge. When he got closer, the first thing he noticed was a piece of rope tied to branch and stretched straight down, like there was a weight on the other end of it or something. The crying sound had died down a bit, and he could hear the low whisper of a woman's voice as well. Benny took a couple more careful steps until he was close enough to peer over the edge.

Twenty-three

THE TRAIL OF THE three Mitch was following led across two more sloughs they had been forced to wade to avoid long detours out of their way. One put him in waist-deep in stagnant, algae-coated water, but Mitch expected that. The farther downstream the men went, the more low-lying and wet the land would become, until eventually it became part of the vast swamps surrounding the Pascagoula River, into which Black Creek emptied. But Mitch was determined that even if these men were planning to go that far, they would never make it. He was going to intercept them and he was going to be waiting when they stopped to meet whichever one was the forth of their party who was paddling that canoe with April and Kimberly in it.

Beyond the last and deepest slough, the tracks entered an extensive area of storm-damaged hardwoods. Mitch knew the destruction was caused by Hurricane Katrina's passage through the state in 2005. While the area around his family's land had been mostly spared, there were pockets of devastation throughout the forest here and there, the worst of them caused by spin-off tornados spawned by the tropical storm. This many years after, those swaths of broken and uprooted trees were utter hell to travel through. Not only were the fallen trunks and broken tops piled haphazardly everywhere, enough time had passed that the second-growth trees taking their places sprung up in rampant profusion. Mitch knew that eventually, the ecosystem would return to normal and much of the undergrowth would be choked out by the biggest and fastest-growing new trees. But that wouldn't likely happen in his lifetime, and until then he did his best to avoid traversing such areas unless absolutely necessary. Today it was necessary though, because those he sought had clearly passed this way, as evidenced by the frequent use of a machete to clear the worst of the obstructions.

A good half-hour had passed as he worked his way into the thicket and still, there were no more distant gunshots after the second blast that seemed to come from the same shotgun as the first. Mitch thought it might be safe to assume that the shots were unrelated to April's captors and he certainly hoped that was the case. But the trail he was following was now leading closer to the creek bank, and suddenly the machete cuts had disappeared. Mitch figured the men must have been concerned about the gunshots as well and were working their way closer to the creek in case there was a problem that involved the other guy.

They had pushed their way through the brambles here without cutting them, attempting to step on briar vines and push them down out of the way. Mitch had to do the same, but at least the three going before him had made it a bit easier by breaking down the worst of it. Realizing it would be tough using the bow effectively in such dense undergrowth, he swung his father's rifle in front of him on its sling and held it at the ready. He could drop the bow and bring the carbine into action at a second's notice if needed, and he was glad he'd made the decision to go back and get it even though it meant losing sight of April. It would do him little good to catch up if he didn't have the means to quickly and decisively eliminate the threat these dangerous men posed.

He was glad their trail was leading closer to the creek, because it might mean they would rendezvous with the canoe sooner. Every minute that April and Kimberly were out of his sight was a minute anything could happen to them. Mitch wanted this chase to be over before something did.

* * *

April pleaded with Kimberly in low whispers to stop crying. She had no idea what was going on downstream in the direction that Wayne had gone. There had been no other sound since that gunshot she'd heard not long after he left, and she guessed at least fifteen or twenty minutes had passed since then. Kimberly had settled down a bit, but was still whining. April could have soothed her by rocking her back and forth, but that was simply too risky in the tippy canoe.

177

She had been focused on quieting her as best she could for the last few minutes when she suddenly got the feeling she was no longer alone. Was Wayne back already? She glanced up to the top of the bank above her, dreading to see him again, but instead was shocked to see a stranger with a heavily bearded face staring down and her and her child. April was so surprised as she recoiled back in shock that she almost lost her balance. The canoe rocked hard beneath her and the rope tugged at her neck, but she quickly frozen and focused her center of gravity as low as possible to counter the roll that would have capsized it if she had not.

"Whoa! Be careful there young lady!"

April regained her composure and looked back up. Judging by the whiteness of the man's beard and long hair that hung over his shoulders, he was at least in his sixties, if not seventies. In his hands, held at the ready but not pointed at her, was a pump-action shotgun. Was this the man who'd fired the shot that sent Wayne off to investigate, and the second unexplained one she'd heard since he left?

"How in the world did you get yourself in such a fix? And with that child too? Be still now and don't you turn that thing over. I ain't gonna hurt you—neither one of you. Were you with that fellow with the bow and arrow?"

"Yes! He's the one who left us tied up. Where is he? He can't be far away and he's coming back any time!"

"He ain't far away, that's for sure. But he ain't coming back neither, don't you worry about that."

"You saw him? Who are you? What are you doing out here?"

"Name's Benny Evans. Yeah, I saw him. I saw him shoot my boy with one of them dad-blamed arrows he had! It's the last one he'll ever shoot though, I'll tell you that. I hope he wasn't your man or something like that, young lady."

"You killed him? Oh thank God! Is your son…?"

"Yeah I killed him; deader than a stump. My boy's okay. That arrow just got him in the arm."

"I'm sorry he got hurt, but I'm glad he's okay though. That man was a murderer. They came into our camp this morning. They left my husband either dead or dying, I still don't know. They were taking me and my daughter someplace downstream."

"Wait a minute, you said 'they?' You mean there's more of them? Where? How many are there?"

"Yes! There are three more that were with him this morning, but please! Cut me loose before this canoe turns over and my baby drowns!"

April saw the man glance nervously around him as he drew a large knife from a sheath on his belt.

"Don't worry, they're not nearby. They're somewhere on the other side of the creek, on foot. I turned my ankle and couldn't walk, that's why the one you shot was taking us down the creek in the canoe. He was going to meet up with them again where we were stopping tonight."

Hearing this, April saw Benny relax a bit. His knife parted

179

the line securing her neck to the branch above and she felt an immediate wave of relief wash over her.

"Hold on now while I find a way to climb down there. I'll cut you the rest of the way loose in a jiffy."

"I am so glad you're here! I can't tell you how afraid I've been for my child! I don't know how I would have gotten away from that man on my own, and especially not all four of them."

"There's a lot of people turned bad since the lights went out, young lady. I don't know where you came from or how you made it this far, but it ain't easy staying alive with all the desperadoes running around that'll do most anything. That's why we're out here. Me and my boy have been in the woods for going on six months."

April had a good feeling about Benny Evans despite his rough appearance. She knew it was risky to trust anyone these days, precisely because of what he just said. But there was just something about him that her intuition told her was okay. He was not like Wayne and his partners, and hearing that Wayne was dead was the best news she'd had since this entire ordeal began. She wished all four of them were dead, but it was enough that she was free of him. As long as she never saw the other three again that was all that mattered.

With difficulty, Benny managed to get down the steep, cliff-like bank the same way Wayne had climbed up, using exposed roots as handholds. He had slung the shotgun over one shoulder to do so, and she noticed the homemade strap was some kind of animal skin, with fur on one side. He was wearing moccasins too that looked like something he'd made himself. There was no place to stand at the base of the bank and the water was too deep here to wade in, so he climbed directly into the canoe, taking care not to upset it as he lowered his weight to the rear seat Wayne had occupied before.

"I hope you don't mind me coming aboard," he smiled, looking at her first and then at Kimberly, who had quieted down now that she could feel her mother's touch again.

"We're delighted to have you aboard, I can assure you," April smiled back at him as she extended her trussed-up hands so he could slice the binding that held her wrists together. When his blade freed her, she threw the cut lashings overboard and asked to use the knife herself to cut away the rest of the ropes holding her ankles, which would have been difficult for him to get to without risking the balance of the canoe. Benny gladly obliged, handing it to her handle first. He kept a respectful distance in the other end of the boat, watching patiently as she finished freeing herself.

The knife was perfectly balanced in her hand, and April couldn't help but notice that it was beautifully crafted and clearly hand-made by a skilled blade artisan. Her father had passed down to her his appreciation of well-made blades through the hundreds of hours of martial arts instruction he'd shared with her, much of it knife-focused. Though Ben's knife wasn't a fighting-style blade and was closer in design to the skinning knife Mitch favored, it was still perfectly balanced and in her trained hands she knew it would be highly effective. That this stranger trusted her with it in the close confines of the canoe made her feel even better about him, though she had already chosen to trust him and believe his story of his encounter with Wayne as soon as he related it. She knew that in part, it was a natural reaction to feel better about *anyone* after being at the mercy of a man like Wayne for most of the day.

With her hands and feet free and Kimberly held close against her breast with one arm, April passed the knife back to Ben. She assumed he would leave now; after all, his son was injured and needed his help and she wouldn't presume to ask more of him. It was enough of a miracle that he came along when he did. She shuddered to think how things would end if no one ever came and she could not find a way to get free of Wayne's ingenious restraint.

"Where were you going, you and your husband, before those fellows came along and did what they did?"

"We were looking for a friend," April said. "A good friend of mine who helped me back when the blackout first happened. He lives on a remote farm not too far from here, but I couldn't find the path that connects it to the creek. He is the son of a game warden, and a real expert in hunting, tracking and everything else to do with the woods. We would be safe there, and he would welcome us in, but I think we came too far downstream."

182

"Sounds like the kind of fellow that would be a good friend to have in times like these. Me and my boy have been making do okay out here for ourselves. But we haven't been any farther upstream yet. We were planning to go, looking for better hunting. In fact we were breaking camp this afternoon, looking to move out before dark. I killed a hen turkey just a while ago, before that fellow with the bow showed up."

"That was the shot we heard then," April said. "That's why he stopped here, because he didn't want to paddle around the bend and run the risk of being seen."

"I reckon not. It wouldn't look good to nobody to be seen paddling down the river with a young woman and her baby girl all hog-tied like that. Say, our camp is just right around the bend. This is a hard place to get out of the boat right here anyway. Why don't we paddle down there and I'll introduce you two to my son. I need to check on him, and then we can talk. Me and Tommy have a canoe too and we can help you get back upstream if you like. We were going that way anyway and I'd hate to think about you and that little girl out here alone. How far up do you think it is to the place they left your husband?"

"I don't know how far in miles, but we've been in the canoe for hours. It'll take a long time to paddle there against the current, if it's even possible. I don't know if he's alive, but if he isn't, I need to bury him. You've done so much for us already, killing that monster, especially. I'd hate to put you and your son at more risk. Those other three are just as bad as he was, and when he doesn't show up where we were supposed to meet, they're gonna be looking for him. And they were probably close enough to hear your shots anyway. If they did, they could be heading this way right now."

"Then we'll get Tommy and throw our stuff in our canoe and go. We'll take both of the boats and head upstream right away. They won't be looking in that direction I don't suppose."

"No, I think you're right. It would be the last place they would look. They're gonna think Wayne took us and kept going downstream to wherever that camp is they were taking us to. They were already unhappy about splitting up, and they thought he wanted to keep us for himself. If you're sure you want to do this, we'll go, but we need to get out of here fast."

Twenty-four

GARY HAGGARD CURSED UNDER his breath as he battled the nearly impossible thickets of briar vines that slowed their progress to a crawl. If not for the two nearby gunshots, he would have hacked his way through these thickets without hesitation, taking a chance of a random encounter rather than creep along at this excruciating pace. But the chances of trouble were more than random now. Two gunshots in the direction of the creek that Wayne was traveling with their prize was simply something that could not be ignored. Whatever he had to do to get there, Gary was determined to reach the banks of Black Creek again and stick to the stream course until they were all back together.

But these briar patches that grew up these areas of blow-down were worse than any he'd ever seen. Patches of blackberry and other thorny vines grew ten feet tall or more, their long, grabby tendrils reaching out in all directions and twisted together in impenetrable tangles. They grabbed at his BDU trousers and shirt, and raked the exposed skin of his face and hands, drawing blood as he impatiently forced his way through them. The worst ones required coming to a complete stop, delicately lifting the vines free of his clothing by grabbing them between thorns as carefully as possible. He would then pass it to Jared, who would duck under and pass it in turn to Paul. It was infuriatingly slow, but the only way to traverse this mess without making noise.

"How did we ever wind up getting this far from the creek?" Jared whispered, equally exasperated and tired of dealing with the briars.

"It's easy to do in woods like this," Gary whispered back. "The way it bends and all these sloughs that run into it. It's hard to follow the lay of the land; a lot harder than in the open country over there. At least in the mountains and desert, you can see where you're going."

"This is like trying to find your way through a maze," Paul said. "Except there aren't any paths, the right way or the wrong way."

"It can't be much farther. We might have veered off a ways, but we're still in the creek bottom. It's just that the farther downstream you go, the wider and wetter the bottomlands get."

"Wayne's the one who's it got easy," Jared muttered. "Just riding the current downstream with nothing in his way and a hot girl to stare at all day. No wonder he wanted to take the canoe!"

"It may be easier, but it's a hell of a lot riskier. You all know that. But women make men do dumb things."

"Yeah, it's like he'd rather take a chance at getting shot

than to leave her behind. I mean, she's fine and all, but I don't know why he'd want to be bothered with trying to keep her. And especially with that baby. Two more mouths to feed and she'll always be looking to get away somehow."

"He'll get tired of her, just give him time. He may even be tired of her by the time we get back home."

"If he hasn't already gotten himself shot," Paul said.

Gary really didn't think that had happened, especially considering the two shotgun blasts were spaced apart by at least 15 or 20 minutes. It seemed more consistent with someone hunting, but even so, the hunter had to be close enough to the creek that Wayne's passing in the canoe might be noticed. If something did happen, Gary wanted to be there to back him up. Knocking that punk out this morning on the sandbar had been a little taste of action, but it took so little effort it was hardly notable. It was nothing like going up against a worthy adversary. And his trigger finger itched as he wormed the muzzle of the AK through the briars. It had been awhile since he'd engaged a real armed tango, and the prospect of encountering that shotgunner gave him that old rush of adrenaline he had been missing lately.

He finally found the end of the blow-down clearing and once again they entered a deeply-shaded area of mature hardwood timber. The winds that leveled the area behind them hadn't touched this area. Gary knew hurricanes were strange that way. Microbursts of intense downdrafts or isolated tornadoes within the cyclone's path would level some houses in a neighborhood and leave others without so much as a lifted shingle. It was the same in the forest, and he was glad to find another of those untouched, pristine areas where travel was once again not only reasonable, but pleasant. They stopped to regroup on a soft carpet of deep green moss in the shade of a giant beech, and after a moment of cussing the thicket they'd just left behind, Gary hushed the others so they could listen carefully. A faint sound drifted through the trees from not far ahead—the sound of running water.

"The creek!" Gary whispered. "Let's fan out a bit and slip up to the bank. I want to be sure no one's there first, then we'll pick our way downstream."

* * *

Mitch hated following three armed men through a tangle like the one through which the trail led. He knew they didn't have any reason to suspect that they were being followed, at least no reason that he was aware of, but still. What a perfect place to lie in wait and ambush your pursuers. They could cut him to pieces with rifle fire in here before he ever saw them. He tried not to let these thoughts creep into his mind as he followed the tracks, but he knew it would be a relief when the trail emerged from this mess. Mitch wanted the space to be able to use his bow if possible, though he knew that odds were, he'd be finishing this fight with his dad's Smith & Wesson AR more than likely.

188

Carrying it at the ready as he pushed through the briars brought back a flood of memories of the times the two of them hunted together. Many times while following up on a covey of quail flushed by Old Charlie, his dad's English Setter, they had busted through briar patches similar to this, shotguns at ready for the fast-action that would follow when the singles burst out of cover in ones and twos. To Mitch at ten years old, it had been a lot more exciting than just trying to kill a few birds. Stalking into the briar patches with his dad on his flank, both their guns locked and loaded and ready in a two-handed, low grip, Mitch had imagined they were at war. The enemy would appear at any second, but they would be ready. He would look out for his dad and his dad would cover him. Together, the two of them were an unbeatable team. On some hunts the imaginary foe would be Viet Cong hidden in the jungles of Southeast Asia. Other times it might be a band of renegade Apaches or outlaw train robbers. No matter what, it was never just quail hunting in Mitch's mind, and thinking back to those days, he really wished now he had his dad with him to cover him for real. This time when he found his quarry, they would be shooting back if he gave them half a chance.

It was a relief when he came to the place where the men emerged from the thicket and entered another patch of real forest. They had not stopped to lie in wait for him and now the conditions were more in his favor for seeing them well before they saw him. The trail across the moss-covered ground was harder to follow, but here and there were still places where a boot had torn the bright green ground cover or overturned a few leaves. Such places were fewer now though than before, and Mitch figured it was because they were moving with more care, for the same reason they had stopped cutting through the briars shortly after they entered the blow-down area. They had heard the gunshots too and were trying to move quietly as they made their way to the creek to investigate.

Twenty-five

BENNY EVANS HAD NO doubt that this woman who said her name was April was telling the truth. Seeing the way that fellow who had tried to kill his boy left her and her little girl tied up, he doubted that she was lying when she said she didn't know the man he'd just shot before today. Benny figured a fellow like that who would try to shoot an unarmed man in the back with an arrow for no good reason would do most anything. And seeing how he believed what she'd said about the man, Benny took her warning about the other three being nearby to heart too.

What she said about going upriver made a lot of sense. Even if it wasn't the direction she wanted to go, it was smart thinking because it would be unexpected by most people. Around these parts, at least before the big blackout, people either floated downstream in canoes or used johnboats with outboard motors if they needed to go upstream for some reason. Even now he hardly ever saw anyone trying to get upriver under their own power, but Benny didn't mind it himself. His granddaddy had taught him how, way back when he was a kid growing up in south Louisiana. You didn't paddle a pirogue upstream anyway—you poled it. Back in his granddaddy's day, nobody had motors on small boats, but they all knew how to pole a pirogue. It wouldn't do to get way off downstream and not be able to get back up, so poling was as natural as paddling in those days, people just lost the knowledge of it, for the most part. Benny wasn't one of them though, and he'd taught his boy Tommy how to use a pole too. It worked in a canoe as well as it did in a pirogue. You just had to have a long enough pole and an eye for reading rivers, so you'd know how to keep your boat where you could always find the bottom to push off of.

Benny Evans liked poling upstream, and in fact, that's how he and Tommy had reached the place they were camped now. Benny always told Tommy that only dead things floated downstream, and it was true. Any thing that fell in the river would get washed along with the current, but it took effort to go against it. It made Benny feel more alive when he made that effort. This whole new lifestyle made him feel more alive, in fact, and even though a lot of it was hard work, he knew it was good for a fellow to live like this too. People had gotten too soft before the blackout. Now they had to harden up if they were going to make it.

As long as he had Tommy, Benny was determined he *was* going to make it. Losing Betsy after nearly fifty years had been hard on him, but at least he wasn't alone. When her medicine had run out and she passed on, Benny and Tommy buried her in the backyard and locked up the house for the last time. The two of them had been ranging up and down Black Creek ever since, hunting and fishing along the way and trying to stay out of sight and out of trouble. They had managed do so for the most part, but Benny knew that what happened today had been a really close call. If he hadn't made it back to that clearing when he did, his boy would be dead. And if those men that the woman warned him about found out he'd killed one of their own, he and Tommy were going to sure enough have a gunfight on their hands. Benny had no intentions of getting tangled up in a shootout like that, so he was ready to do just what April suggested and get upstream on this creek as fast as possible. He just had to get Tommy and their own canoe and gear first. He knew Tommy wouldn't be expecting him to come around the bend in a canoe, and Benny didn't want to surprise him and risk getting shot, so when he got close he whistled a signal.

"It's so he'll know it's me and that it's all right," he whispered, when April gave him a look like she thought he was crazy for making loud bird sounds. When a nearly identical whistle from downstream replied right away, Benny told her it was the call of the bobwhite quail.

"I had no idea," April said. "I think I've heard that before, and I knew it was some kind of bird, but I'm a city girl."

"I can tell you are, young lady, but you've survived this long, so eiher you're doing something right, or somebody up there is looking out for you. There he is." Benny nodded in the direction of a clearing that came into view a few seconds later as the canoe rounded the bend. He knew his boy would be completely shocked to see him paddling another canoe, and one with a pretty young woman and a little girl in it to boot.

"It's okay, Tommy!" he called, careful to keep his voice low as he steered the bow into the mud bank. "This here's April. And her little girl...."

"Kimberly," April said, as she held her baby in her arms and greeted Tommy. "I'd get out, but I turned my ankle so bad this morning I'm afraid I can hardly walk."

"I had a little trouble myself, Miss April." Tommy had a hunting rifle cradled awkwardly in his arms as he kept pressure on his wound with a blood-soaked, wadded-up T-shirt.

"I know. I'm sorry that happened, but I'm sure glad that man is dead."

"Tommy, I know you're hurt, but we've got to get out of here, son. April here says there's three more of them fellows just as bad as that one laying there, and they ain't far away either."

As he said this, Benny saw April staring at the dead man with little visible emotion. He couldn't imagine how scared she must have been, after what they did to her child's father and then the way they took her and that little girl. Benny figured the two of them wouldn't have lasted long after those fellows had their fun. It was just a miracle really, that he shot

194

that hen turkey when he did, and it was that gunshot that led to the bad guy being dead instead of the young woman and her child.

Benny walked over to the body and removed the holstered automatic pistol. Then he found the man's sheath knife and after searching his pockets, some spare magazines for the pistol and a large folding Sypderco that April said was hers when she saw it. He was ready to go then.

"We ain't got time for that," Benny said when he saw Tommy turn to try and finish packing up the tent. Let's just throw everything in these two boats and go. We'll sort it out later. With any luck at all, they'll naturally think we went downstream from here and they'll head that way."

"I don't think I can be much use with a pole with this arm like it is, Pop."

"That don't matter, you just worry about keeping that bleeding stopped. We'll tie April's canoe to our stern and tow it. It won't make no difference at all. You can hardly feel the weight of a canoe, towing it like that. I can manage the poling for a while by myself. As long as we get around a couple of bends up I think we'll be all right and I can rest when I need to. But now ain't the time for talking about it. We've got to do it and now! And we've got to be as quiet as possible about it too."

* * *

195

INTO THE RIVER LANDS

As he slipped quietly closer to the sound of moving water, Gary Haggard was pretty certain that he was still moving directly towards the source of the two shotgun blasts. Now that they were almost to the banks of Black Creek again, he was also fairly certain that whoever fired that shotgun had to have been close to the creek as well. He had his finger resting lightly on the side of the trigger as the kept the AK in front of him, ready for action. A quick glance to either side confirmed that Paul and Jared were staying even with him on either flank as he closed the distance, and both of them were ready to engage as well.

Gary hadn't heard anything else besides the two shots. No voices or other human sounds, just the two widely-spaced blasts that interrupted the birdcalls and other natural sounds of the woods for a few moments, before all returned to normal once again. There was no way of knowing exactly where Wayne was in the canoe. For all he knew, he could be a mile farther downstream by now, but Gary knew he had to check this out. It was aggravating, and all of it was Wayne's fault for being so stubborn, but it was too late to argue with him now.

He finally caught a glimpse of water through the thick screen of greenery, and motioned for Paul and Jared to wait while he advanced the last few feet. If there was anyone near the bank, he wanted to be sure he saw them first before they had a clue that he and his friends were there. Gary crouched low and took two or three slow steps at a time, stopping to look and listen in between each move. When he finally had a full view of the creek, he was almost certain it was the right spot because directly across, in the forest on the opposite bank, was a good-sized clearing that looked man-made and looked like it had been there for a long time. The clearing was grassy but free of briars and brush, and in the middle, there was a well-used campfire ring surrounded by large logs that seemed positioned in such a way to favor sitting around the fire and talking.

Whoever fired those shots was probably staying here, and Gary wondered if they had been here when he and the other guys had passed this way going upriver just a couple of days before. He knew it was possible, because just like today, they had been traveling on foot and had made many direct shortcuts between the long bends of the channel. This site was in just such a bend and that's why they had missed it. Chances were, they could have been as far as a half-mile away when they trekked by this place on their upstream hike and whoever was here would not have been aware of their passing.

Gary watched until he was sure no one was hanging out at the edge of the clearing right now, then he motioned Paul and Jared to his side. When they got there, he said he wanted to go just far enough downstream to find a place to cross the creek unseen. He wanted two of them to stay here, concealed on the bank on this side to cover him if anything went wrong over there. He was still suspicious that those shots somehow involved Wayne. But even if they didn't he still wanted to know who fired them and why. It wouldn't take long to find out. Once Paul and Jared were set up in a good spot to cover the clearing, Gary slipped downstream, keeping in the cover of the woods until he found a spot that was as good as any to cross.

Twenty-six

MITCH CAUGHT A GLIMPSE of movement among the trees ahead of him and immediately stopped to watch and wait. After a few more seconds, another movement confirmed that he had visual contact with at least one of the men. The creek bank was just ahead, just past the spot where he'd seen one of them working his way forward in a low crouch. Mitch stalked closer, until he saw that all three of the men he was following were squatting there on the bank, apparently discussing something. He knew that he had to be near the spot from which the gunshots came, and he was sure the three men were watching the river to see if they could determine the source too.

He was too far away to hear anything they were saying, as they were talking in low whispers anyway. It was too risky to try and get closer at the moment, as the mature forest here was relatively open. He settled in behind a fat tree trunk to watch and wait, and soon one of the men left the other two, making his way downstream. Mitch recognized him as the one who'd hit David with the rifle butt. The other two stayed where they were, both of them now lying prone with their rifles pointed in the direction of the creek or the bank on the other side. Something there had attracted their attention and that was why the one had left alone. Mitch figured the other two were waiting here on this side to cover him, so he was probably going to try and get across to the other bank. That they were splitting up was good for Mitch. He decided he would wait until the other one was across the creek to see what they were up too, and then deal with these two while they were separated. But first, he wanted to get a look at whatever it was over there that got their attention.

The safest way to do that was to backtrack a bit and circle around, flanking them from the upstream side, opposite the direction the third man had gone. The two were focusing all their attention on the other side of the creek anyway, so it wasn't hard for Mitch to pull this off. Keeping behind tree trunks as much as possible, he moved slowly until he was near the edge of the top bank some seventy to eighty yards upstream from the two watchers. From this new vantage point, Mitch could see a clearing across the creek and this explained their actions. It was obvious that someone had been camping there. The remains of a recent campfire were visible from where he was too, and these guys had seen it and intended to check it out. Mitch scanned the woods on the other side for movement but didn't see any signs of life. If whoever fired that shotgun had been camping there, they were gone now or else very well hidden.

Mitch waited where he was until he saw the one man who

had left the other two sneaking quietly through the trees just downstream of the clearing. He was approaching with caution and a decent stalking technique, and Mitch figured he was probably the most experienced of the four when it came to hunting skills. It was good that he was on the other side, because those skills made him more dangerous and it would be easier to deal with him alone.

The minutes seemed to pass like hours as he waited for the man to make his next move. He was careful; Mitch had to give him credit for that. When he was at last apparently satisfied that the clearing was deserted, Mitch saw him step into the open with his AK held at ready. A hand-signal telling the other two to "hold on" was his only deviation from the task at hand. Once he reached the fire pit area in the campsite, Mitch saw him freeze and then raise the AK to his shoulder. Pointing at something lying in the grass, he turned back to face the two covering him and drew a finger across his throat. Someone over there was dead, so the shotgun had indeed been fired from there. But who did the shooting and who was shot? Mitch figured it probably didn't have anything to do with April and the other man who had taken her and Kimberly. There was no sign of the canoe or any other reason to believe they had stopped here. They would likely have had time to get past the spot before those shots were fired too, even with one person paddling. At least that's what Mitch wanted to believe. But after the man in the clearing was certain he was alone there, he once again faced his waiting partners and this time called out to them. What he said renewed Mitch's fear for April and Kimberly's safety and put a whole new twist on any hope he had of finding them quickly.

"It's Wayne! He's dead!"

When the other two replied with a barrage of questions, the man across the creek waved them to silence and motioned them to come on over instead of answering. Then he turned and started scouring the ground around the edge of the clearing, obviously looking for footprints or any other clues. Mitch saw the two on his side of the creek get to their feet and start moving downstream, headed for the place the first one had crossed.

Mitch was determined not to let that happen. Now was his chance to eliminate these thugs; probably the best one he would get. He slid the AR sling around so that the rifle was on his back and switched back to his bow, nocking an arrow as he set out to follow them. He had no more time to waste tracking these three, so he wasn't about to let them out of his sight again. If someone had shot the man who took April and Kimberly, then whoever it was must have continued on downriver with them in the canoe and he needed to catch up. But he wouldn't know for sure until he examined the tracks in that clearing himself. He had no desire to wait for these men to move on before he did that, so taking them out immediately was his best option. After what they had done, he would show them no mercy. The world would be a better place without them.

He quickened his pace to close the gap as he followed, having little fear they would detect his presence as they were focused on getting over there and finding out what happened to their dead friend. Mitch waited until the first one entered the creek wading into chest-deep water, holding his rifle high overhead. Feeling his way along the bottom to keep from stepping into a deep hole, he would not be looking back at his partner who was still on the bank. Mitch drew his bow and took aim at the second one, who was still squatting down to remove his boots while the first one was about halfway across. He had a clear shot at the side of the man's neck, and he watched in satisfaction, as the flight of his arrow was straight and true. The man clutched at his throat for a second before he fell forward on his face in the mud, but Mitch was no longer focused on him and already had his second arrow on the string and his bow fully drawn. With only his head and shoulders exposed above the water and a small backpack high in the middle of his back, this one presented a more challenging target. Mitch knew from past experience that head shots worked just fine with a bow and arrow, at least with the heavy broad heads he favored. He centered his aim on the base of the man's skull and let the arrow fly, but at just that moment, his target stumbled and his head went under. Mitch's arrow sliced into the empty water beyond where his head had been, a clean miss that left him grabbing for a third arrow to follow-up. Fortunately for Mitch but not for the man in the creek, his sudden dunking made him completely unaware of the deadly missile that had missed him by inches. When he regained his footing and turned back to mutter a curse to his partner he thought was right behind him, he didn't have time to comprehend what had just happened and why the other man was lying in the mud. The third arrow that left Mitch's bow that day caught him just above the collar bone, passing through his neck and into the water beyond, almost in the same trajectory as the one that missed. The man collapsed and his head went under again, a stain of blood visible in the current just moments later as Mitch nocked a forth arrow and made his way down to the bank.

* * *

When Gary Haggard found Wayne's body and knelt beside it to see what happened, there was no question as to the cause of death. His friend had caught a load of buckshot square in the chest, and from close range, too. Gary figured it had to have been the second shot they'd heard, but why was Wayne here, on the bank and not in the canoe? Since the canoe and the woman and her little kid were nowhere to be seen, Gary figured it was pretty certain that whoever had shot Wayne had taken off with them. If they had, then it had been nearly and hour and whoever it was had a good head start with the help of the current. Gary didn't give a damn whether he ever saw that girl again. She was the reason Wayne did something stupid and ended up dead after all, but he did want to find whoever did this and make he or them pay for what they did to his buddy.

That was going to be a challenge, but they had to go downstream anyway to get home. He began by looking around the body and the rest of the clearing for footprints. There were none from the woman, so he doubted she ever got out of the canoe. He found a lot of man-sized tracks other than Wayne's that had no tread pattern and seemed to be made by moccasins or something similar. These crisscrossed the mud and sand in the clearing and around the edges and Gary couldn't tell whether they were made by one man over the course of several days or by more than one in a shorter period of time. He checked the fire pit in the middle of the clearing and when he kicked over the coals and put his hand near them, he could feel the heat from the buried embers. Someone had only recently put out the fire, but the pile of coals and the extra wood heaped nearby suggested that whoever had camped here might have been here several days or even longer.

Gary went back over to Wayne's body. If Paul and Jared would hurry up, they could quickly bury him in the soft sand if they worked quickly. Though they'd had their differences on occasion, he and Wayne had been friends for a long time and he hated to leave him lying there like that for the coyotes and vultures. His fallen comrade had been stripped of his weapons; the Glock 20 and its spare magazines, his compound bow and his Ka-Bar were all gone. His backpack with his other gear was missing too, but Gary figured that was probably still in the canoe where he had tied it to a thwart when he shoved off. Gary checked his pockets for the Spyderco folding knife he had taken from the woman when she was forced to drop it and found it missing too. He had nothing else on him of value.

Gary glanced downstream in the direction from which he expected Paul and Jared to follow him over here from the other side. He wondered what was taking them so long and he was going to be aggravated if they had gone farther out of the way to look for a shallower place to cross. Both of them had been cussing under their breath every time they'd had to wade a slough. He scanned the bank opposite where they had been watching and saw that they were not there, so he figured they should be coming along any minute.

He returned to the creek's edge and examined the drag marks in the sand. It was obvious that a canoe had landed and shoved off from here, but it was odd that it had done so in two different places. Could there have already been another canoe here when Wayne and the woman came along, or had the stranger that took it after killing him have pulled it back up on a different part of the bank for some reason before leaving? It made sense that the stranger or strangers may have arrived here by canoe, considering that they were camped right on the riverbank. He also had to consider that there was some slight possibility that the woman had not been lying about others in her group traveling the river separately. Could it be that whoever shot Wayne knew her, and maybe she had left willingly with them? It made sense that they wouldn't hang around here long if that were the case, since she knew that he and Paul and Jared were paralleling the creek on foot as close to its course as possible.

Gary couldn't be sure what any of the tracks or drag marks meant, but what he what he *was* sure of was that they'd left here by canoe. And to his mind, that meant that they were somewhere downstream. With the way the current was running, he figured they might already have covered two or three miles since leaving here. He and Paul and Jared may not be able to catch up to them while they were paddling, but he figured they would eventually have to stop somewhere. All he wanted was to get them within rifle range. When he did, he would kill them all, the woman and kid too. They had caused him more than enough trouble already.

He'd had enough of waiting for Paul and Jared too and he was going to let them know it. He stormed back downstream to the place where he'd crossed the creek and stopped in his tracks at what he saw on the opposite bank in the mud. It was Paul, facedown and still in a totally unnatural position. As soon as he realized what he was seeing, he heard something sing past his right ear at high speed, followed by the solid whack of an impact. A glance in the direction of the second sound revealed a heavy wooden arrow buried in the trunk of a tree six feet behind him. Gary leveled the AK in the

207

direction from which it seemed to have flown and pulled the trigger. A ten-round burst from the converted weapon would force the attacker to keep his head down and prevent him from shooting another arrow—that is, if one of the steel-jacket rounds didn't find him or her by chance and eliminate the problem.

Twenty-seven

APRIL STIFFENED WITH FEAR on the canoe seat at the sudden sound of machine gun fire ripping through the silence just a short distance away downstream. Benny paused mid-stroke with his pole in the canoe in front of her from which he was towing hers. His son, Tommy, the bleeding from his arm finally under control, also turned to look back as the staccato echoes of rifle shots faded away.

Before anyone could speak, there was another short burst, then another and another, followed by several single shots in rapid succession.

"That sounded like an AK-47," Benny whispered. "In fact, I know it was. You reckon that fellow's friends have found our campsite already?"

"Yes," April whispered back. "It's got to be them. One of them was definitely carrying an AK. I didn't realize it was full-auto though." April thought back to the brief education Mitch had given her about firearms during their time together. Before all this happened, she would have thought any black gun that looked as menacing as the patrol rifle his father used in his job as a game warden was a machine gun.

But Mitch had told her no, that despite the common appearance of full-auto assault rifles in movies involving drug dealers and other criminals, they were rare in civilian hands. He told her they were highly illegal without a special permit and most of what people thought of as "assault rifles" were actually semi-auto lookalikes. He did say the AK-47 could be converted back to the original design fairly easily, however, but not many people would risk it because it was a serious federal crime to do so. The semi-auto versions were popular and common though, so April guessed that with no one to enforce restrictions like that now, it was probably happening a lot. To men like those four who had taken her and Kimberly, laws of any kind meant nothing, so she was hardly surprised.

"I don't know who they could be shooting at with that thing though," Benny said. "Maybe just firing it off up in the air because they're scared after finding their friend I shot."

"Yeah, that's probably got them fellows pretty jumpy, Pop." Tommy agreed.

April wasn't so sure about this. Those men didn't seem to be the type to scare easy from what she'd seen. Whatever the reason for the machine gun bursts, the sound told her they were nearby and that she'd been right to urge Benny and Tommy to leave immediately. She hoped she was right about going upriver, and she was sure glad Benny had the knowledge and skill to get them out of sight going this way against the current. Paddling would have been a lot slower, and hopeless for her alone with Kimberly. But Benny had managed to get them around two big, sweeping bends of the creek before they heard the machine gun fire. With any luck at all, the three men would assume whoever took her and Kimberly and the canoe had gone the other way. Maybe they would take off that way in hopes of catching up. But whatever they did, she didn't care as long as they didn't find her and her child and she never had to lay eyes on them again. To that end, she urged Benny on in their quest to get upstream as far and as fast as possible.

"We need to keep going," she insisted. "They are still way too close for comfort."

"I agree," Benny said. "I know I don't want nothing to do with them fellows, especially with them toting full-auto rifles. They're gonna be itching to shoot anything that moves after finding their buddy with that load of buckshot in his chest!"

"We're gonna give them the slip, going this way, Pop. I think she was right about that."

"Yep, it was the right choice all right. Like I always said, dead things go downstream, and we'd end up dead for sure if we went down that way now. Life is upriver, boy!"

"Wish I could help you out with the poling."

"Don't worry about that, son. I've got it. I've got to do something to keep myself young and spry!"

April smiled at the exchange between this gentle father and his grown son. She knew she was incredibly fortunate that Benny had found her when he did, and that he had a good heart, unlike so many of the strangers she had encountered since the lights went out. She knew there had to be more good people just trying to survive after their world collapsed around them, but lately, they sure seemed few and far between. She'd seen so many of the other kind who were taking advantage of the misfortunes and weaknesses of others that she had about lost her faith in humanity. But she instinctively knew Benny and Tommy were good folks; simple country folks with enough knowledge of the outdoor life to be able to adapt to the sudden and severe changes the solar pulse had wrought. They didn't need to hurt others to get what they needed to survive, because they were already pretty self-sufficient before the grid went down anyway. April figured that in a lot of ways, these two were much like Mitch and his family.

With Benny's ability to pole the canoe upstream at a reliable and efficient pace, she began to have hope once again that she would find Mitch. By looking more carefully, maybe she would see the path to the Henley land that she had somehow missed on the way downstream. But first, she knew they would reach the sandbar where David had been left for dead, but probably not before the end of the day tomorrow, because even with Benny's skill at poling, upstream travel was far slower than downstream. April dreaded what she would find there. She had little hope that he would be alive, if he still was when they'd left this morning. Kimberly was too young to be fully aware of what happened to her father, but she would know something was wrong and she was already looking for him expectantly. April would somehow have to hide from her the truth; while they were burying her daddy in some lonely shallow grave lost in this vast river land forest.

* * *

Mitch couldn't believe his bad luck. After he made his way across the creek and started stalking his way upstream to the clearing, the third and last surviving man of the three he'd been trailing stepped into view in front of a tree. Still unaware anything was amiss regarding his companions; he presented a wide-open and clear shot just as he came within sight of the place the other two had crossed. Mitch had seized the opportunity and quickly drew his bow and released. This last man, who was clearly the most cautious and experienced of the three, once he knew something was up, would be a much more difficult and dangerous target.

And that's exactly what happened. Mitch had just released his arrow as the man spotted the fallen figure of the first one he'd killed on the opposite bank. Recognition that something was way wrong about the way his friend was lying face-down in the mud caused the man to instinctively flinch and duck, and Mitch's arrow never even touched him. It was rare that Mitch missed a shot, and when he did, it was almost always due to something out of his control.

Before he could get a follow-up arrow on the string, the

213

man realized what had just happened and dropped to his knee and unleashed a burst of automatic rifle fire in his direction. Mitch dove to a prone position and crawled behind a fallen log as bullets cut through the leaves and tore bits of bark off trees and branches all around him. He was quite sure that the man had not actually seen him; he was just laying down fire in the vector he knew the arrow came from. He was trying to force Mitch to keep his head down and keep him from getting off another shot, and it was working; at least for the moment.

Mitch knew he couldn't wait to see what happened next though. His dad had taught him basic gunfighting tactics that he had learned both in his dangerous backwoods law enforcement job and in his former days as a Marine. Mitch had no doubt his opponent had similar knowledge and skills, based on the way he'd seen him check out the campsite. If he was right, the man would make a move soon, thinking he had every advantage with the firepower of his automatic rifle. Against an opponent armed only with a bow, he could lay down a heavy barrage of fire to prevent a counterattack as he moved in for the kill. But the one thing he didn't know was that he wasn't going up against just a bow. Mitch slid the AR-15 sling around his shoulder as he stayed pressed as close to the ground behind the log as possible and placed the longbow in the leaves beside him. He had just brought it to his shoulder when the next burst of AK fire came his way. This time it was only three rounds. And a few seconds later, another short burst of the same, and then another. The man was coming closer now; ducking from the cover of one tree trunk to the next as he fired his short bursts each time he moved. The bullets were ripping high over his head and Mitch was sure his attacker still hadn't seen him and didn't know exactly where he was. But he would be on top of him in a moment where he couldn't miss. He couldn't afford to let him get that close. When he stepped out again, Mitch opened up with a double-tap of the semi-automatic AR and saw the man spin and fall, crawling for cover behind the base of a big oak after he hit the ground. Mitch fired two more rounds and was certain he hit the man in the thigh or hip and likely the lower leg too before he dragged himself fully behind the tree. He heard him suppress a scream of rage and pain, and he knew his enemy must have been surprised indeed to get hit by rifle rounds when he thought arrows were all he had to worry about. Mitch kept his sights on the tree, ready to fire again at the first sign of any attempt to return fire. The distance between them at this point was barely over thirty or forty yards. Any attempt to get closer or move laterally would be extremely risky if the man was still able to shoot back, but Mitch wasn't sure he was. The high-velocity 5.56mm rounds could do a lot of damage even with a leg shot, and with any luck at all he might have even hit the femoral artery.

He watched and waited. It was a familiar game, just like hunting, where a wounded animal would sometimes freeze in hiding for many long minutes before either making a dash to escape or succumbing to blood loss. But Mitch didn't have all day. In fact, the day was about to run out and the low angle of the sunlight filtering through the trees told him it would be dark in an hour, and there would be too little light to read tracks even sooner. After a good fifteen minutes and still no sound or movement from behind the tree, Mitch knew he couldn't wait any longer. He began slowly backing away, keeping low and never taking his eyes off the big oak tree. He would go back into the forest downstream and then make a wide circle around where the man was hiding and make his way to the campsite from the other side. He knew if he was careful, the wounded man would never know he had left. Mitch absolutely *had* to find out what happened to April before it was too dark to see. Finishing this guy off could wait until later; if he didn't bleed out on his own by the time Mitch found the information he needed.

Twenty-eight

JASON BURNS HAD FINALLY convinced Mitch's sister, Lisa that there was no point in trying to follow him down the trail of the those guys he was tracking. He knew Mitch wouldn't want her to be anywhere near danger like that if it wasn't necessary, no matter how much his little sister might want to give him a hand. He said their time was best spent trying to find David, who had mysteriously vanished after Jason and Mitch had last seen him unconscious on the riverbank. But though they scoured the area for clues, there was no trace of David other than a single set of footprints leading straight into the creek. They looked on the other side for indications he had crossed it, but on that side was the big sandbar that was already covered in tracks made by April, David, the four strangers, and then Mitch. It was a confusing jumble of footprints that had frustrated Lisa for the better part of the afternoon and she still had no idea where the injured man could have gone after he apparently woke up on his own and walked into the creek.

They had eventually given up while there was still enough light to find their way back to the farmhouse, but Lisa had insisted on returning early the next morning, this time alone with Jason, so they could search farther up and down the banks on both sides and try to pick up a trail David might have left. Mitch had not returned, of course, and Lisa was still arguing that they should have followed him yesterday, because he might have gotten into a situation he couldn't handle, having four bad guys to deal with all on his own.

"I'm telling you, Lisa, we did the right thing! We might have just messed things up and made it worse if we had followed. Mitch knows more about this stuff than all of us put together. He's going to be okay. You'll see. I'll bet he gets back early today, and with April and her kid too."

"I hope you're right, I'm just worried about him, that's all. The whole time he was with April before, it seemed like he was in danger. Now, she comes out here, apparently looking for him, and here he goes again."

"Well, it's not like he had much choice. He would have done the same for any woman and child he saw taken by men like that."

"Yeah, I know, I was just hoping we could all just lie low on the farm and avoid these kinds of situations. You know how risky it is. You were beaten half to death yourself."

"I was, and if it weren't for Mitch and April coming along when they did, I would have died there on the side of that road. And no telling what would have become of you and Stacy."

"Well, since we can't catch up to Mitch or the men who

took April, the least we can to is keep looking for David and not give up until we find him. If Mitch does bring her back, she's going to be glad to see him. And the little girl will need her daddy."

Lisa and Jason were back at the spot where David had last been seen shortly after sunrise, and this time Lisa planned to methodically search both banks in the upstream and downstream direction. She didn't think David had gone far, and she knew he wasn't deliberately trying to elude them, but she had heard her father talking about manhunts for fugitives in the woods and some of what he said stuck with her. One of the oldest tricks around to throw off trackers and dogs was to wade into a stream at one point and then travel a considerable way either up or downstream before exiting. It would at least slow pursuers down, while they looked for the exit point, and if it was done well might throw them off the trail entirely.

The hours went by as they scoured the banks this way, first on the same side of the creek they knew David had started from, then on the opposite. Around a bend downstream, they found a place where a canoe had landed and saw more confusing footprints, but none they could positively identify as David's. After giving up there, Lisa just wanted to continue downstream at least a mile or two, reasoning that if he had floated or swam a greater distance than expected once he entered the water, then downstream was the only logical direction he could have traveled. They were about to give up and go back to the house when both of them heard the sound of voices from somewhere even farther down the creek.

"We'd better check that out," Jason said.

Keeping several yards within the forest but still close enough to see anything that moved on the water, the two of them slipped quietly along, carrying their weapons at ready. The voices had stopped momentarily, but then they heard them again. The tones were low and could not be at all far away.

"I think whoever it is, they're coming closer," Lisa whispered.

"I think you're right. Listen! Did you hear that?"

"Yes." The sound was unmistakable for anyone who had spent much time around a creek like this in the summertime. It was a the clank of a paddle or some other object agains the hull of an aluminum canoe. Lisa knew for certain that's what it was, but it was unusual for anyone to be coming upstream against the current.

"Maybe it's Mitch bringing them back in the canoe the men took," Jason said.

"Maybe, but we'd best not take a chance. Let's just wait right here and keep down until we see."

They did not have long to wait until sure enough, a canoe suddenly appeared from downstream. It was not Mitch and April though. Two men occupied it, both with long hair hanging over their shoulders and thick beards that obscured most of their faces. The man in the bow was sitting, doing nothing, while the one in the stern, who looked much older, judging by his nearly white hair, was wielding a long pole. The man clearly knew was he was doing, and the canoe shot upstream with each push as easily as most people could paddle one downstream. But something else surprised Lisa and Jason even more than the ease with which the man was making headway against the current. Tied to the other end of a taut rope that stretched from the stern of the canoe, was a second canoe in tow. And in it was a woman Lisa and Jason both immediately recognized as April, sitting there holding a small child in her arms.

* * *

April was becoming more despondent with every day that passed. It had been nearly two weeks since that day that Lisa and Jason led her and Benny and Tommy back to the Henley farm, and still Mitch had not returned. Nor did they have any idea what became of David.

When Lisa and Jason had hailed her from the bank after figuring out she was not a prisoner of the two rough-looking men towing her canoe, she had been shocked to learn that Mitch was looking for her. It seemed incredible that she had been so close to him that day that Wayne and the others took her and Kimberly, and yet she never knew it. She never knew that even as she was so terrified of the uncertain future that lay ahead of her in the hands of those men, Mitch was hot on their trail and doing everything he could to rescue her and her child. But if he was that close, so close that he had seen the whole thing as it unfolded, then where was he now? What had happened to him?

After sitting on the bank discussing the whole scenario with Jason, Lisa, Benny and Tommy, they concluded that all the gunfire they'd heard the day before in the vicinity of the place Benny had killed Wayne must have been connected to Mitch. He must have caught up with the other three and there must have been a gunfight. April wanted desperately to find out, but there was no way she could put Kimberly at further risk. Crossing paths with Lisa and Jason meant she had found her way, and Lisa said the farm was not all that far. April couldn't walk anyway without assistance, and even after nearly two weeks her ankle still hurt when she spent too much time on her feet.

The very next day after they were all safe at the Henley farm, Jason and Benny set out for the two-day round trip by canoe to the campsite where Benny and Tommy had encountered Wayne. They were hoping to find Mitch or at least determine what had happened during all the shooting they'd heard, but they found no one alive in the vicinity.

Wayne's body was lying where he had fallen when Benny shot him, and scavengers had already found him.

"Dogs or coyotes, most likely," Benny said. They found another dead man just a short distance downstream, lying in the mud, his eyes picked away by vultures. If he had been carrying weapons, someone had taken them.

"I'd bet anything he was one of the four," Jason said.

I'm betting you're right," Benny said. "Look, that wound in his throat wasn't made by a bullet. It's cut too clean. It looks to me like he was killed by an arrow, and it either got lost or whoever shot it picked it up. I'll tell you something else too; that was one clean kill—a perfect shot if I ever saw one."

"It had to be Mitch," Jason said. "He's incredible with a bow and arrow. But if it was, where did he go?"

They searched and searched but didn't find the answer to that question or any clue to the whereabouts of the other two. Benny offered his best guess though.

"You know, when I first found April and her little girl, she said we ought to go upstream because she knew those fellows had a camp somewhere downstream they were taking her to. It was good thinking on her part, and for sure wouldn't have been what they expected. I'm thinking your friend, Mitch wouldn't have expected that either. I'm thinking that he came along and saw the dead one I killed and saw the canoe was missing too. He probably thought somebody else took the two of them downriver. Most people would think like that."

"And if Mitch didn't kill the other two, they would be looking down that way too, right?"

"Yep."

"How are we ever gonna know then?"

"I reckon we ain't, really. If them fellows did get the best of Mitch in all that shooting we heard, his body could be almost anywhere within a half a mile of here, the way gunshots carry so. It would be like looking for a needle in a haystack out here in these woods. And going downriver would be just as useless. Those river bottom swamps down there just get wilder and wilder the closer you get to the Pascagoula. I'm thinking all we can do is is just go back to the house and wait. If he *is* alive, he'll show up eventually when he doesn't find any sign of April down that way."

When Benny and Jason returned to the farmhouse with news of what they found, April knew Benny was right. Mitch wouldn't give up until he exhausted every possibility in his search, if he was still alive. When they described the other dead man, April knew it was one of the other two, whose names she did not remember or care to recall. It was somewhat encouraging to know that the man had definitely been killed by an arrow, and she had no doubt it was Mitch who did it. But with the other two unaccounted for and all that shooting noise, she knew something could have happened to him after that. What if the other two men managed to get the better of him? After all he was one against three, and at least one of them, that Gary guy, was a real tough customer, and armed with a machine gun. April had to face the possibility that Mitch was dead, and that he died trying to save her.

SCOTT B. WILLIAMS

The thought tore at her soul as she waited, and waited and waited, each day and night passing interminably slow on the Henley farm. She had her Kimberly, and for that she was grateful. But Kimberly didn't have her father and April didn't have the one she'd thought about almost constantly for the entire seven months since she'd last seen him. She spent hours rocking her child on the porch of Mitch's family home, sitting with her in the antique caneback rocker that he'd told her had belonged to his late grandfather. After all she'd gone through and all the risks she'd taken to finally get back to this place, the one she'd come here to find was no longer here and might never return. Tears rolled down April's face as she sat and rocked, despite how much she tried to keep her focus on the fact that for now at least, she and Kimberly were safe.

Twenty-nine

MITCH HENLEY WAS NOT a quitter and had never been one to give up before achieving the goals he set for himself. But he was at a complete loss and continuing to search where there were no clues to be found was getting him nowhere. It had been almost two weeks since he'd set out downstream from the place he was certain April had last been. Mitch had examined the body of the leader of the four men—the one who had been killed by a shotgun blast from some mysterious stranger. His weapons had been taken and Mitch had found the keel marks in the creek bank mud where two canoes were launched. He had been certain at the time that April and Kimberly were in one of those canoes. He had also been quite certain that whoever left with them had headed downstream. It was the logical conclusion at the time, but now he questioned every decision he'd made that day.

First of all, in his haste to try and find a sign of April before dark, he'd left the man he'd exchanged gunfire with and circled around to the campsite. He had been sure that he'd wounded him badly, judging by the way he fell before taking cover behind a tree, but with no way of knowing whether or not he was truly incapacitated, Mitch couldn't risk getting closer. Nor did he have time to spend hours playing a waiting game with darkness fast approaching. Once he determined April was indeed nowhere nearby and saw the canoe marks, he left immediately to follow the creek downstream. His hope was to catch up to whoever took April and Kimberly wherever they stopped for the night.

But he never found that place, if indeed there was one. Though he followed Black Creek all the way to the edge of the Pascagoula swamp lands where it joined Red Creek before emptying into the big river, he never saw the two canoes. He checked every sandbar and other probable landing sites on both sides of the creek on the way down, but found no marks left by a canoe hull. Mitch knew it was possible to paddle long distances without stopping and that someone bent on doing so could have gone that far in one marathon stretch, but he doubted they would. Burdened with a captive who had a small child, they would have almost certainly stopped somewhere along the way, and likely many places. The farther he traveled downstream, the less likely it was beginning to seem that they had come this way at all. If Mitch had found the slightest bit of evidence that they had, he would have continued on in his quest, even if it took him all the way to the coast. But as it was, he had to admit that he might have made a bad decision. He had utterly failed in his attempt to rescue the woman who believed in him enough to leave the city and come back to Black Creek to find him.

Things must have gotten really bad in Hattiesburg for her and David to take that risk, traveling all that way with Kimberly. It was heartbreaking knowing they had come so close, and that he had actually seen her and yet still could do nothing to save her.

Mitch knew that he would return to search again, as many times as it took to try and find out what happened. But he still had his sister and the others back at home to think about, and he knew that after all these days they would be really worried considering what Jason told them he'd set out to do. With a heavy heart, he made his way slowly back upstream, still looking for anything he might have missed. When he reached the campsite again and what remained of the two bodies left lying there, he spent even more time trying to decipher what might have happened. But there had been at least two good rains since the day those two men died there, and any sign he might have missed before would be much more obscure now.

While there, he also found the tree where the man he'd exchanged gunfire with had been hiding. The man was not dead there as he had dared to hope, and if he had indeed been wounded, Mitch could find no evidence of it. He considered trying to track him down, but decided there was little point. Following that man would not lead him to April, and since he wasn't there when the one who had taken her in the canoe was killed, he wouldn't know what happened to her either. The man was long gone anyway by now and the trail was cold. It would take him days to catch up, if he ever did, and he felt that he needed to get back to the farm sooner than that.

He continued on upstream in the direction of home, still stopping to check sandbars and mud banks along the way for anything unusual. He didn't rule out the possibility that the canoes had gone upstream, but he really doubted it. That doubt disappeared, however, when he came to sandbar where someone had clearly camped recently. It was about five miles upstream from the place where the shootings happened, and as Mitch scoured the sand looking at the washed-out, poorly defined tracks, he saw faint keel marks above the high water line that indicated two canoes had landed here. *Did they go upstream after all?* It sure looked like there was a good possibility of it, though he couldn't be sure it wasn't someone else who'd landed here. It was certainly enough to give him hope though, and for the rest of the journey back to the farm he was on high alert for anything unusual. He crossed the creek when necessary to check a sandbar on the opposite side, and he stopped often to look and listen. It was during one of those stops that he heard someone approaching through the dense forest.

Mitch nocked an arrow and waited behind a tree. The sound was certainly that of a human and not an animal, he could easily tell by the heavy footfalls. Whoever it was, he or she was being quite careless and making no attempt to travel with caution. Mitch tensed as he caught a glimpse of movement first and then saw the outline of a man. The man had stopped when he came to a small rotting log, and Mitch saw him squat down in front of it and begin tearing away the rotting wood, as if he were digging for something. Apparently he found what he was looking for, because next he began desperately shoving something in his mouth with both hands. Mitch bent and twisted to get a better view through the foliage. The man was eating grubs he'd found in the log. His clothes were torn to shreds and his hair was matted and covered with mud, like most of the rest of his body. It took him a minute to see through all the dirt, but then Mitch realized the man he was looking at was David! *April's* David!

* * *

David tried to run from him when he first called his name and revealed himself, but Mitch doggedly pursued him until he stumbled and fell. When he attempted to reassure him and remind him who he was, and that they had met seven months ago when he led April to the church sanctuary in Hattiesburg, David just looked at him with a blank stare. He didn't know who Mitch was and April's name meant nothing to him either. Even when Mitch brought up Kimberly, David showed no sign of recognition. Clearly the blow from the rifle butt had done serious damage. He wondered why he was out here and in this shape when the last time he'd seen him, he was unconscious, under a tree and Jason was supposed to be going back for help to get him to the house. But for whatever reason, he'd apparently spent all those days since crashing through the woods, eating bugs and drinking from mud holes. But at least he was alive. It took some doing, but Mitch finally persuaded him to come along with him. He told him that where he was going, there was plenty to eat and that he would be safe.

While they walked, Mitch tried every thing he could think of to jar David's memory, but nothing seemed to work. He didn't know much about amnesia, but he'd heard that it was sometimes temporary and sometimes much more long-lasting. He wondered if David would ever be normal again, and then thought that his memory loss might be merciful, as the man wouldn't have to suffer with the knowledge of what happened to his child and the woman he loved. Unfortunately for Mitch, that pain would never go away and he would never forgive himself for not acting immediately when he first saw what was going on there on that sandbar. He'd been worried that he would put them in more danger by acting rashly, but now realized it would have been worth the risk considering what happened anyway. For now, all he could do was take David to the house and check on Lisa and the others. Then he would return to look for more evidence of those two canoes even farther upstream, in case that was really the way they went. He knew he would never be able to stop searching, even if he had to break it up into short forays in between taking care of his other responsibilities to the others.

When he and David finally reached the hidden path that led from the creek bank to the Henley property, Mitch was shocked to find two canoes upside down and partially concealed in the canebrake where he and his dad usually kept their own canoe. Looking at them carefully, he was quite certain that one of them was the one that had been on the sandbar when April was captured. He tried to verify this with David, but David said he had no idea who they belonged to. Mitch slung the bow he'd been carrying in his hand onto his back and brought the AR-15 around to the ready position for the approach to the house. Had whoever taken April somehow gotten her to tell them where the house was? Could they have done something to Lisa and the others as well? Mitch's mind was racing with the possibilities as a rush of adrenaline flowed through him. Fortunately, David seemed to understand the need to be quiet, and he obediently followed Mitch without uttering a word.

When he reached the barn on the back edge of the yard, Mitch told David to stay put while he stalked closer to reconnoiter. Using his old path he'd used as a child to sneak up on his parents at the house, Mitch slipped into position where he could see the porch and the front door. The house seemed intact and he saw nothing out of the ordinary at first. Then the front door opened and an old man with long white hair and a huge, bushy beard stepped out of his house. Mitch instinctively raised the AR to his shoulder and placed his sights on the center of the man's chest. *Who was this stranger and what had he done here?* His finger was on the trigger, but he was not going to fire just yet. He had to know more; especially whether or not the old man was alone. The door opened again and someone else stepped out. Mitch saw that it was his sister, *Lisa*! She seemed to be fine and did not seem to be afraid of the old man. In fact they seemed to be carrying on a conversation as he watched them walk to the rail of the porch. He lowered his rifle and his focus shifted to the door again when it opened and someone else walked out of the house. It was a woman, and in her arms was a small child. The woman walked to his grandfather's rocking chair and sat down, apparently equally at ease with the old man as was his sister. Mitch blinked and rubbed his eyes, straining his vision to make sure it was not playing tricks on him. *Could it be? Was it really her? It didn't seem possible, but it had to be and it didn't matter how!* Mitch stood and stepped out into the open yard. *April and Kimberly were alive!*

About the Author

SCOTT B. WILLIAMS HAS been writing about his adventures for more than twenty-five years. His published work includes dozens of magazine articles and twelve books, with more projects currently underway. His interest in backpacking, sea kayaking and sailing small boats to remote places led him to pursue the wilderness survival skills that he has written about in his popular survival nonfiction books such as *Bug Out: The Complete Plan for Escaping a Catastrophic Disaster Before It's Too Late.* He has also authored travel narratives such as *On Island Time: Kayaking the Caribbean,* an account of his two-year solo kayaking journey through the islands. With the release of *The Pulse* (2012), *The Darkness After* (2013) and *Refuge* (2014), Scott moved into writing fiction and has many more novels in the works. To learn more about his upcoming books or to contact Scott, visit his website: www.scottbwilliams.com

Made in the USA
Middletown, DE
11 August 2022